Molly hesitated before she went into the kitchen. There was a tingling feeling in the air. *I am the First Visitor. There will be Three in all.*

Something is happening, she thought. I've been pretending it's just ordinary, but if I go in the kitchen now, I shan't be able to pretend anymore. She walked stoutly through the kitchen door.

"I am hoping you can help me," said the man. He sat down, and as he did so Molly caught out of the corner of her eye a shivering, hardly visible, forked-lightning effect. "Your application was most impressive."

Molly gave him a puzzled, guarded glance, saw what he held out to her, and gasped. "My advertisement! How—?"

"Any words may take wing when the heart yearns to soar beyond its bounds," said the stranger softly. "You have offered yourself to us for the work. You have been told what will be asked of you? The dangers?"

"There is a child," said Molly haltingly.

"And you will cherish him for so long as need be. He will be brought to you at a fitting hour," said the stranger, rising from his chair. Then he turned and was gone.

Out of the Ordinary

ANNIE DALTON

HarperKeypoint
An Imprint of HarperCollins*Publishers*

Out of the Ordinary
Copyright © 1988 by Annie Dalton
First published in 1988 by Methuen Children's Books Ltd, London
All rights reserved. No part of this book may be used or reproduced in any
manner whatsoever without written permission except in the case of brief
quotations embodied in critical articles and reviews. Printed in the United
States of America. For information address HarperCollins Children's Books,
a division of HarperCollins Publishers, 10 East 53rd Street, New York,
NY 10022.

Typography by Joyce Hopkins
First American Edition, 1990

Library of Congress Cataloging-in-Publication Data
Dalton, Annie.
  Out of the ordinary / Annie Dalton.
    p.   cm.
  Summary: Fifteen-year-old Molly, who lives in a turbulent, single-
parent household, is asked by mysterious, otherworldly visitors to
protect an enchanted child from great danger.
  ISBN 0-06-021424-4.—ISBN 0-06-021425-2 (lib. bdg.)
  ISBN 0-06-447081-4 (pbk.)
  [1. Fantasy.]   I. Title.
PZ7.D16940u   1990   89-39787
[Fic]—dc20   CIP
                                                     AC

Harper Keypoint is an imprint of Harper Trophy, a division of
HarperCollins Publishers. First Harper Keypoint edition, 1992.

To my mother

"Three uninvited guests arrive.
Honor them and in the end will be good fortune."

From the I Ching, or Book of Changes

Contents

Out of the Ordinary

CHAPTER ONE

Molly Casts a Spell to Banish Ordinariness

Just as Molly had finished her paper round, the rain, which had been soft and drizzling, began to hurtle down, bouncing back from the pavement to sting her hands and legs in spiteful, half-frozen pellets. Before she had reached the end of Rustling Lane, where the posh and not-so-posh houses met in an uneasy truce by the park, the rising March wind was driving steely gray drops against her so furiously that she was gasping. As always, by the end of her round, she had walked herself into a daze, her feet trudging her homeward without interference from her brain, her stomach growling for its missed supper.

She was soaked through, her shoulder aching from the weight of the *Bradley Free Echo* bag slung across it, but as she turned away from the park out of the worst of the wind, heading for Vine Street and home, she glanced compulsively toward Albert Villas on the corner to see if the "other house" was there today.

Sometimes she couldn't see it at all. Sometimes she could see it only as a sort of ghostly underlay to Albert Villas, though even then it seemed that the "other house" was more real rather than less, with its white octagonal tower, its glowing gardens, its glimmering, tantalizing air of being within sound of the sea, of being fringed by forest. Today, even by just a quick glance from under her sodden fringe, Molly could see that the other house was enjoying perfect weather. Lucky things, she thought.

She didn't know why she could see things that other people couldn't. It seemed to be one of the things she was stuck with, like a sensible face and frizzy red hair and big feet, but unlike them it didn't show. It couldn't be confided in anyone either. It belonged in her most private life, along with the voices she sometimes heard talking or singing as she was falling asleep, and the silent music that started up from somewhere deep in her own bones when she suddenly knew just what was going to happen next in her own life, almost as if she were watching a film for the second time.

Turning her back firmly on the sunlit tower, Molly registered that as usual she had one paper left over. She was supposed to be given exactly the right number for her weekly round, so she guessed she must regularly be missing someone though no one had yet complained. She always kept the extra paper in case someone spotted her guiltily ditching it in a litter bin. Delivering *Free Echos* was tedious and very badly paid but it was the only job she had found.

Hauling herself up the last few hundred meters of Vine Street, which was not strictly a street at all but a steep cobbled hillside of old, mainly dilapidated terraced houses, she squinted through her dripping frizz at the Tamara's Stars column, to see what the universe might be planning for her. She hoped to be ready for it whatever it might be:

"You are a survivor with hidden powers but you don't know it yet."

This was disappointing as well as confusing. What good to Molly were things she didn't yet know? She read the next star sign too. She suspected Maureen, her mother, was a little fuzzy about her date of birth, because Molly's father had walked out around then. Molly thought she might have been born on the cusp which gave the universe a second shot on her behalf:

"Unexpected visitors bring undreamed of opportunities."

On the face of it this was more promising. Except that it was not so very unexpected in Maureen Gurney's household for there to be anything up to half a dozen unexpected visitors at any one time: Cliff's motorbike cronies, friends of Sean's who hung around for days playing computer games, social workers bringing yet another disturbed foster child to haunt their nights noisily with its terrors. There could also be any number of neighbors whose sugar had run out, washing machines had broken, husbands had deserted them, or any random combination of these disasters. As a result, Molly often spent nights on the lumpy sofa downstairs instead of in her own beloved attic bedroom. There were hours of tea and sympathy while the family supper dried out beyond recognition in the oven.

There was also a steady parade of scrawny fledglings unable to fly or feed themselves, bronchitic hedgehogs, abandoned two-week-old kittens needing to be fed every two hours with a dropper and cosseted by the stove, and any number of unwanted puppies or stray injured cats and dogs whom no one but Maureen Gurney would dream of taking in and nursing back to health. Molly had once opened the cupboard and found a startled but re-cuperating hen.

Maureen, Molly thought, seemed to be atoning for several hundred past lives spent in roaring vice and wickedness. In her present incarnation even a fly would be fished tenderly out of her tea and grieved over if it failed to recover. Maureen, Molly thought, was kind to the point of being barmy. Congenitally unable to make her mouth form the word "no" to anyone.

"Except me," she said, scowling, swinging her *Echo* bag down the side alley so that it scuffed against the wall, pushing open the gate to number 223, sniffing suspiciously at the absence of supper smells. "She always manages to say no to me all right."

As she reached the back door, the rain redoubled its fury. It became a freezing curtain she had to force herself through. The wind rose higher, howling melodramatically. The Equinox, thought Molly. It's the time when everything changes over. Perhaps something will happen. Undreamed-of op-portunities, it said.

Dripping on the kitchen floor, she began to peel off her sodden things, shivering. Her hands had turned as red as raw beef with cold. Except for a convalescent guinea pig grumbling gently in its straw beside the old-fashioned heater, the kitchen was empty. The only sounds in the house were the electronic bleat of a computer game in progress in her brother Sean's room on the first floor, and canned studio laughter from the TV.

Drying her hair with a towel, she wandered plaintively into the living room, where Cliff was slumped in front of the television set, his motorcycle jacket still on and zipped up to the neck, giving him a huge-shouldered, stiffened, mechanical look, like the Tin Man in *The Wizard of Oz*.

"Where's Mum?"

He dragged his attention irritably away from the screen. "No idea." It was a quiz show. Molly watched nervously for a moment: a sweating, rapidly blinking man in a tight suit got the answer wrong and she averted her eyes quickly, but Clifford brayed with satisfaction.

"Have you had supper?" Molly interrupted again.

"Yes, of *course*," he said furiously, his eyes refusing to unstick themselves from the screen. He wanted her out of the room so he could lose himself in the television world again. Only TV or riding fast on his motorbike gave Clifford any apparent pleasure. To everything else in his world, Clifford said a violent "No," supplying a necessary balance in the family of Maureen Gurney, perhaps. But

8

Molly remembered him when he was younger and different and sometimes wondered if the real Clifford had been stolen away, leaving behind instead this angry blank substitute. He had left school last summer and showed no sign yet of finding a job. Sometimes she felt frightened of him.

She gave up on Cliff and went to find Sean, following the electronic gibberish up the creaking stairs to the room where he and his zombie friend Vince were manipulating computer paddles intently in near darkness. The screen flashed and glittered. Cartoon figures the color of fizzing sherbet danced across in dizzy formation, exploding other figures, or else being exploded into fragments of sherbet-colored light, according to the skill of the player.

"Where's Mum?"

Dee doodle dee doo—crowed the computer. The game was over.

"That was my best yet," said Vince, without emotion. He combed his hair and stuck the comb back into his breast pocket.

"Don't know," said Sean, without looking up. He was putting another disc into the machine.

"Did she leave me some supper?"

"How should I know? Look in the fridge, can't you?" said her brother. "Oh yeah," he added, remembering. "She did say to tell you to make scrambled eggs or something. She's gone to her class."

Of course! Maureen had suddenly got into self-improvement and tonight was her first Open University class.

"What did you have for supper?" she asked suspiciously.

"Fish fingers. Shut up, will you?"

"This'll be my best yet," intoned Vince. Molly relaxed. She would rather scramble eggs for herself every day of her life than even look at a fish finger. Then another thought struck her.

"Where's Wayne and Chantal?" It was much too early for them to be in bed.

"For Pete's sake, shove off!" Sean was tapping his fingers menacingly on the space bar, frantic to be rid of her. "Old Thingy the social worker came at tea time and took them back to their mum. Which means we might get at least one night's sleep before the next load of snotty orphans is washed up on the doorstep."

Molly went out quickly and closed the door. Her eyes stung. She was rather fond of Wayne and Chantal. She was used to Chantal creeping breathily into her bed at night when she had a bad dream, warming her small icy feet on Molly's large warm ones. "Tell me a story, Moll," she'd say, all shaky and snuffly from her nightmare. It had been nice, telling stories to Chantal in the dark.

Wayne was slower than his sister and somehow, Molly felt, a sadder child. Sometimes he had the worried look of a tired old man. But this morning he'd been giggling like mad into his cereal when Molly did her impersonation of the guinea pig for him. "Bye-bye, Baby Bear," she had said, kissing his upturned laughing face, all smeared with breakfast honey. She hadn't known she was saying good-bye forever.

She went downstairs and began cracking eggs into a bowl, stern with herself. Never look back. Never regret, that's what Maureen had taught her. You had to look forward and hang on to your dreams. You had to be ready for what the universe might be planning for you.

The wind was still rising, wailing down the chimney and rattling every loose window frame in the house. In strong winds, the straining fabric of the old house vibrated and thrummed like a tormented musical instrument. The Gurneys' house was at the top of Vine Street, almost level with the moors outside the town. From the front of the house you could see row upon row of houses and factory chimneys stretching away down into the valley and up the other side. But from the back, the house

11

looked over surprisingly wild, neglected gardens and orchards, and several acres of overgrown cemetery belonging to a church long fallen into disrepair. Molly thought this brambly unexpected place, green and haunted by squirrels and field mice and hedgehogs and wild birds—and even a few foxes in recent years—gave the house a subversive, secretive side to its nature. On a night like tonight it had a wild, unstable feel. By morning it might have spread its wings and flown far into the hills away from the dull little northern town. She sympathized.

She sat at the kitchen table eating her eggs and toast, listening to the wind shriek and the tap drip, muttering back at the guinea pig and wondering why the house was trying to get away and where it was trying to get to. Then she caught herself wondering these peculiar things and wondered instead if she would ever acquire the normal obsessions of a fifteen-year-old. From time to time she did try to get interested in pop singers. She dutifully stuck up one or two posters to put Maureen's mind at rest. She even wrote Andy Noyce's initials on her pencil case and circled them with a heart in felt pen. Andy was a fairly human-looking sixteen-year-old who had accidentally won her admiration for knowing the names of stars and planets, and then as swiftly lost it again by criticizing an Ursula LeGuin

12

she was reading on the bus. As far as she could make out, he was unable to respect the book because it did not end either in nuclear holocaust or with one of the two lone survivors on a barren planet murdering the other one—his recipe for a good read.

On the jacket of his current library book Molly had read the following:

"The Planet Earth is now a poisoned wasteland fought over by two warring tribes. The Urgs are sworn enemies of the Morgs...." Still, at least he could read. It was no use though. Despite the lie on her pencil case, Molly's heart had never really skipped a beat over Andy Noyce, though pretending it did from time to time meant she could hold up her end of cloakroom conversations with Sophy and Kate. Her trouble was:

"My trouble is," Molly said, taking her plate to the sink and washing it up, "that I know there is something more, something else. And it's nothing to do with school or TV or anything I can explain. But I don't know where to start looking, and if I did I wouldn't know what I was looking for."

Someone had kicked the cat's dish and scattered sinister liver-colored bullets over the floor. Molly opened the door to the large drafty pantry where the broom and the brush and dustpan were also

13

kept, and remembered how when she was small and had first begun to read for herself books like *The Lion, the Witch and the Wardrobe,* she kept dashing hopefully into all the family's wardrobes and cupboards, longing to find that *this* time she had really been transported into a magical other world. She swept up the cat biscuits. "Huh," she said, contemptuous of herself. Her trouble was that she was fifteen years old and quite a few months and she still hadn't changed. She was still a hopeless dreamer, a ludicrous dreamer with large feet all too solidly on the ground and frizzy red hair ruthlessly chopped by Maureen to chin length every six weeks. She also had a round, healthy, ordinary face. She was, Molly thought, quite weighed down with ordinariness, like an extra dose of gravity; and she had a talent for nothing whatsoever. Her teacher told her kindly that she might be a nurse one day if she could only concentrate a little more. "You obviously have a way with people." But this was Maureen's training rather than Molly's nature, as Molly herself well knew. Molly didn't want to be a nurse. She would be a terrible nurse. She thought she would be terrible at almost anything you could think of.

Molly's painful feeling of wrongness, of oddness, which she supposed she must always have had, had been growing stronger lately. Something that, again, she couldn't name was wrong or off-balance in some way. "Probably just my life," she said glumly. As if her life was somehow only another of her mother's rummage-sale finds that could never quite be made to fit, something inside Molly was always too big or too small for the circumstances she found herself in. Sometimes both within the space of minutes. In math, chemistry and P.E., she shriveled and shrank like a woollen sweater boiled with the tea towels by mistake. In English, on the rare days when they did something really beautiful like *Romeo and Juliet,* the entire school building wasn't large enough to contain the brimming shining Molly she became. And when she was daydreaming...

The other day it had got out of hand. Something really peculiar had happened, something that she could never possibly tell anybody. They were supposed to be writing notes in a humanities lesson. So far, Molly had learned about the near-extermination of the Aborigines, the North American Indians and the Jews. They had done the Bomb and Famine (Andy Noyce absolutely *shone* with missionary fervor in humanities), and now they were doing the destruction of the Amazonian rain forests. But Molly just couldn't bring herself to concentrate on the ozone layer or whatever it was. Secretly she was trying every way she could think of to shut out Mr. Parfitt's voice and the horrors he intoned with what she felt was a distinctly paradoxical relish in her century's all-too-manifest inhumanity—when something happened to her hand. Very rapidly and quite without her permission it began to write the strangest words, just underneath where the ozone layer left off. At the same time she had that growing tingling feeling again, but it was much more powerful than she had ever known it to be before. Whatever it was that was happening to her was as irresistible, wild, clear and compelling as though an underground spring or stream had suddenly burst through into the stale prison of the classroom and with it birdsong and the damp sharp smell of forest trees. The words seemed to Molly very beautiful as she wrote them and mysterious like a dream or a fairy tale. And like the best dreams and fairy tales they were also disturbing and elusive. She couldn't quite capture or contain this bubbling magical outpouring. What actually appeared on the last page of her exercise book was only some kind of poem. What clamored in her head was more like a song. She thought it was meant to be a riddle, but at the same time it was a piercing, aching lament as if the riddle didn't itself know its own answer.

16

Speak I cannot but silent sing.
Love made me but grief I bring.
Grief broke me and flung me wide,
My curse to mirror all they hide.

One self flew like a bird o'er the sea.
But it has forgotten the true name of me.
Angel or monster, woman or tree,
Ah none of these is the true name of me—

Once this eccentric communication began it was quite unstoppable. It flowed inexorably on out of the exercise book and sprawled over every scrap of rough paper she had in her possession. All she could remember now was the part about the young lovers who were forbidden to marry and so chose to die, predictably enough calling down a curse upon the kingdom with their dying breath. Then there was a lovely part about some mysterious Keepers, or was it Watchers, who saw everything that had happened and remembered it and each night they gathered up all the broken fragments of the unhappy speaker in the riddle— all but one, which could never be found, so that each sunrise all the poor cursed fragments flew apart again:

17

Until what was lost is found
What was broken mended
What was cursed be blessed
And the enchantment ended.

And all the time Molly was scribbling away like someone bewitched, she had the most frustrating sense that there were at least five or six other versions of this riddle or legend simultaneously available, like TV channels, each different from the other, even flatly contradictory, yet each would somehow have conveyed the same wrenchingly sad truth about—something. What? Could there be a separate truth for each of the broken pieces of the riddle? Whatever could it be that was broken?

But at this point the bell rang and she had to scramble to get to the lunchroom with Sophy and Kate before all the french fries went and so the mysterious voice was silenced. Later she couldn't even find the scraps of paper she had written most of it on. She hoped she hadn't handed it in to Mr. Parfitt by mistake with the stuff about the rain forest and the ozone layer. It was a shame anyway, because it had sounded just like the sort of story she loved to read. She did wonder who the lovers were who had died. The part that peculiarly stuck in her head was the part about flying over the sea

18

like a bird. For some reason this reminded Molly of her father, whom she only knew through the rather confused and confusing medium of Maureen's stories about him. There were times when her mother made him sound like someone gorgeous in a film. The kind of person Kate and Sophy would probably moon over.

"Oh, his face," Maureen would sigh, when she was remembering him on one of her wistful days. "And his lovely hair. And how we did used to laugh. You mustn't ever think he was all bad, Moll. It's just that life wasn't always kind to him."

But at other times, from Maureen's darker hints and unfinished sentences, Molly was mainly relieved she hadn't known him. Yet she could still remember that when she was a very little girl, badly wanting a daddy of her own, she used to dream night after night that she flew over the sea to find him in whatever land it was he was now supposed to be (her dream helpfully supplied palm trees, hot sand, camels), and by magic she always did find him. And always in the dream he knew her at once and she knew him and they ran toward each other joyfully. But she always woke up before she reached him.... She was rambling again. Daydreaming and rambling.

"I've got to stop dreaming and *do* something,"

she scolded herself. "But however will I know what the *right* something is to do?"

The guinea pig chittered hopefully in its box and Molly absently answered it in her best guinea pig dialect. Impressed, the guinea pig was inspired to new shrilly virtuoso experiments of its own. "Guinea pigs impersonated," Molly murmured. She began to laugh and then, as suddenly, froze. Next, in a whirlwind of excitement, she hurled herself at the dresser drawer, banging her hip painfully on a chairback, searching through tangles of string and old gas bills for paper and pen. Finding what she wanted, she settled herself at the table, pen in hand, entranced by her own unexpected brilliance. For she had realized suddenly that she had certain very good down-to-earth talents. She hadn't been Maureen Gurney's daughter for over fifteen years for nothing. There were things she could do, and if she could do them here then she could do them elsewhere. She was going to get herself out of her rut of ordinariness. She would find herself a holiday job next summer. She could put a card in the post office. She could even advertise in *The Lady* or something. She'd be sixteen next summer. She began writing quickly before her beautiful idea lost its shine:

CAPABLE RESOURCEFUL GIRL [she wrote], GOOD WITH CHILDREN AND ANIMALS. CAN COOK PLAIN FOOD.

The guinea pig rustled in its straw, rummaging for the last gnawed end of carrot. "Unnh Unnnnh Unnnh," it warbled lovingly in anticipation.

WILLING TO TRAVEL, she wrote, listening to the rain hammering at the windows and pouring down the overflow.

"Oh," she whispered, "I know there's something. I could almost reach out my hand and touch it now."

She stared at her scrap of paper so fiercely it seemed to shimmer. A restless longing rose up in her so violently that for a moment the shabby kitchen blazed with the power of her imagining. She grabbed the pen again and wrote so fast that the writing flew over the paper, seeming to pour magically from her pen:

QUESTS UNDERTAKEN [she wrote]. LOST THINGS FOUND. ENCHANTMENTS BROKEN. DANGER NO DETERRENT....

What's the use, what am I doing? She came to herself slowly, the glow in the kitchen subsiding, the spell fading. Slowly, lamely her pen scrawled: VERY RELIABLE.

What's the use? She wouldn't let me. She always needs me. She'll have had half a dozen foster children by summer. And there's the French student. And she says we might have to get a lodger....

21

In a burst of furious misery and resentment she tore up her crazy stupid advertisement and quickly threw it into the blazing stove. Her unhappiness had taken her breath away as if she had walked suddenly into an icy opposing wind.

There was a small but hungry silence. Even the wind stilled. Then there was an explosive flare as the flames took her words and licked them into flickers of red and gold.

Somewhere in the house a door slammed and a blast of cold air blew around her feet. She found herself shivering.

"Don't be silly," she whispered. "Nothing's happened."

CHAPTER TWO

The Storm Like the End of the World

By ten, Molly had done all her homework, had had several more conversations with the guinea pig and was ready for bed. Her mother was not yet home. Clifford had roared off on his bike and Sean and Vince had gone to Vince's house.

The storm was getting worse by the minute and Molly was feeling less and less eager to climb the stairs to her attic room, where she knew from experience the amplified sound of the rain and wind would sound as if the end of the world was about to burst mightily upon her, like something out of one of Andy Noyce's books. So she had a bath to delay the evil moment, as Maureen would say, and wrapped hugely round with an old dressing gown of her mother's was making herself a hot milky drink, when she heard someone knocking at the kitchen door. With a surge of relief that her mother was back home and she would not, after all, have to brave the stormy end of the world alone in her attic, she padded on her clean bare feet across gritty linoleum to let her in. At first all she could see was darkness and the lashing of wet laurel.

"Mum?" she called, looking up and catching her breath at the chaotic shapes the wind was tearing out of the sky. A lopsided lump of blue-white moon sailed briefly between torn and towering clouds and then vanished. But feeling deeply uneasy she shut, locked and, as an afterthought, bolted the door. Then she jumped with fright.

Sitting in Maureen's favorite old chair by the heater, rain dripping off her tattered old black coat onto Maureen's cracked and long-suffering lino, was an upright but nevertheless very old lady whom Molly had never seen before in her life.

"It's a terrible night," the old lady observed. Molly was still gaping and found herself trembling slightly all over with the shock of this sudden visitation. But she was her mother's daughter and well trained. There could be any number of sensible explanations, she told herself.

"Are you one of Maureen's friends?" she managed to say at last. The old lady smiled with immovable calm but didn't reply. Molly felt she had been impolite. Perhaps Maureen had invited her round, forgetting she would be out. Yawning and shivering in her outsize dressing gown, Molly said, "I'm afraid my mother's out at the moment. Can I get you anything?"

"I'll take a drop of the ginger wine your mother keeps in her dresser," said the old lady. "I would not like to get the ague at my time of life."

She talks like a book, thought Molly. But she obviously knows Maureen all right. And the contents of the dresser!

"Would you like to take off your coat so I can dry it for you?" she asked, setting the glass of wine on the table within the old lady's reach. The old lady shook her head and, almost as a continuation of the same movement, also shook out the skirts of her ancient black coat, as if to show that now it was scarcely wet at all. For a second something shivered out at the hem, like forked lightning from behind storm cloud. Molly blinked. She was imagining things.

The old lady sat forward, holding out her veined brown hands to the heat of the stove. She had not touched the glass of wine, Molly noticed, but seemed curiously content, looking around the big, shabby kitchen and, Molly saw with discomfort, at Molly herself with a bright penetrating gaze like a small fierce bird sizing up the landscape. Molly was confused by her visitor. Little and old and ragged as she was, she wore an air of stern authority. But something else had entered the kitchen with her, some disturbing current that tingled and sang and seemed to want Molly to remember something. *But she's just an old tinker woman in that dreadful old coat and that dead-hen thing on her head. And she looks like a tough old hen herself, sinewy and windburned like someone used to being outdoors.*

The silence was getting uncomfortable. Molly supposed she should make conversation until her mother returned but she had no idea what to say.

"I have knocked on the doors of many fine households," said the old lady at last. She spoke in her strange, serene singsong, but her eyes settled on Molly with a bird's sudden fierce impersonality. "Only you had the kindness to let me in by your fireside. That is always the first test. In my experience it is the most significant."

"Oh dear," said Molly awkwardly. This must be one of Maureen's batty down and outs.

"A night like the end of the world," continued the old lady, smiling at Molly strangely as if they

26

shared a joke. "A night unfit for the world's lost creatures. The *unbelonging* must care for each other, as we always have done." She settled back in the chair and closed her eyes as though exhausted. Molly thought she got the message.

"I'm sure my mother wouldn't want you to be out in this weather. Shall I make you up a bed? Now Wayne and Chantal have gone, there's a spare room." Her eyes filled suddenly and her heart felt a twinge at the thought of those small empty beds.

"Thank you, but I will remain in this chair," said the old lady, stately as a queen. "Nowadays I sleep but little. All I wish for is to spend a stormy night beside your hearth."

Despite herself, Molly was enchanted. She could almost imagine herself to be in a fairy story. If only it were true. She could think of three wishes straight off, no problem. But she was only Molly Gurney with the extra dose of gravity and this was only one of Maureen's stranger acquaintances. "Shall I fetch you something to eat," she asked, "before I go up to bed?"

"A morsel of the bread and cheese you have in your cupboard," said the old lady, a little slyly, Molly thought, as she fetched the loaf and the crumbled remains of the Red Leicester and put a little on a plate. Still the old lady made no move to

27

sample either the food or the wine, but she smiled at Molly, a strange secret smile.

"Did you know there are some people who can travel between the worlds?" she said, very softly.

"No, really? Are there?" said Molly too politely, her stomach tying knots in itself with anxiety. This old lady was mad, no doubt about it.

"You can sleep without fear," the old lady said with sudden sympathy. "Do not wait up for your good mother." Harmless, thought Molly, relieved.

"Okay," she said, trying to make her smile natural. "I should go to bed really. School tomorrow." She began her retreat to the kitchen door. Then she thought of something. "Are you sure you wouldn't like to watch television?"

The old lady's forehead contracted. After a pause she said very deliberately: "I think I will not watch it. I like best my own visions." But she seemed a little puzzled, Molly thought.

"Okay. Well, 'bye then. Nice meeting you," she said.

The old lady nodded and closed her eyes, but then snapped them open at once and moved forward vigorously in her chair so that, once again, out of the corner of her eye, Molly had the illusion of a kind of localized forked lightning shivering out from the folds of her dilapidated old coat.

"I am the First Visitor," she pronounced, her voice suddenly ringing and resonant and young. It was as if the old lady had brought the energy of the storm into the Gurneys' kitchen with her, or was herself a part of it. For a moment her presence filled the room dangerously. Then she sank back and said in a more normal voice, "There will be Three in all." The kitchen came back into focus. Molly rubbed her eyes.

"Okay," nodded Molly again, backing and smiling till her face ached. "Well, 'bye then." As a *fruit cake,* she said to herself, toiling up the worn stair carpet to her attic. As a *fruit cake.* More of that and she'd have magicked a few old vegetables and sent me off to the ball in a gold turnip to meet Prince Whatsit.

She cast off her dressing gown and fell into bed, shivering violently as the cold from the sheets struck her skin. *Oh I wish I'd said good-bye to Wayne and Chantal. Oh no, it's two periods of math and two of P.E. . . .* And then she slept at once and dreamed that Wayne and Chantal were trying to find their way back to Vine Street but the storm had washed away the little white stones they had dropped to mark their path.

CHAPTER THREE

A Fragrance of Sea and Forests

Molly woke to a gentler fall of rain. Overnight the storm had apparently blown itself out. She got dressed quickly and went to find Maureen to explain about the old lady in the kitchen. But it was already later than she thought. Maureen was halfway down her first cigarette of the day and throwing tea bags into the large brown pot. The guinea pig was in full voice, whistling deafeningly for its breakfast. But the old lady was nowhere to be seen.

"Has she gone then?" asked Molly, peering round.

"For heaven's sake drag a comb through that bush, Moll," said her mother irritably, wreathed in blue smoke. "Has who gone?"

"The old lady who came to see you. She was out in that storm and she didn't have anywhere to stay the night. I said it was all right to stay here. Didn't you see her when you came back last night?"

"No," said Maureen vaguely, "but I don't think I came in the kitchen. I was so beat after all that thinking they made us do, I just fell straight into bed and died. Did she say what her name was?"

"No," winced Molly, beginning to tug the comb painfully through her frizz. "And I'd never seen her before either. But I couldn't say no. It was an awful night." She began to giggle, remembering how very peculiar the old lady had been. "She was really batty though, Mum. Like someone in a story."

Maureen, distracted, had wandered, not listening, to the pantry. "Oh Molly," she exclaimed, annoyed. "Who's tramped all this stuff in here after all I've said. As if it isn't hard enough to keep this great barn clean."

"What?" said Molly, her heart sinking. Why did Maureen always seem to think she was responsible for everything that went wrong in this house? She followed the direction of Maureen's accusing cigarette.

On the linoleum immediately in front of the pantry door was a bright drift of sand. As if jeweled, it glinted under the electric light.

"That isn't the sand from the sandpit," said Molly

defensively. "That's soft and damp like brown sugar. This is dry and sparkly gold. The sharp sort, like sea sand. And I didn't put it there, honestly."

"Well sweep it up," muttered Maureen. "Because I most certainly didn't put it there either." Then in one sudden and surprising movement she turned and put her arms tightly round her daughter, hugged her so hard it hurt and then as quickly released her. "Moll, I'm sorry," she said. "You know I'm awful in the mornings. Come on, forgive me. We'll do another take, shall we?" She clapped an imaginary film director's clapperboard and said, "Maureen and Molly Gurney have breakfast. Take two."

Molly grinned at her painfully, feeling confused. The irritation was familiar to her. The apology and the remorse were not. She began sweeping up the sand anyway.

"Oh *leave* it, silly. Come and have breakfast," said Maureen. "You'll miss the bus."

"Good," said Molly, sitting down and buttering away. "Because it's two periods of math and two of P.E."

"Ouch," said Maureen, laughing. She wasn't usually sympathetic either. Molly had suspected for a long time that she thought sympathy to daughters weakened their moral fiber.

"Where do you think the old lady went?" Molly

asked. "Do you think she was a tramp? I was hoping she might turn out to be my fairy godmother." She grinned to show it was a joke. Her colorful fantasy life had once been a sore point between them.

Maureen sighed and poured out mugs of tea for them both. "Perhaps she could have coughed up the money to have the roof done then," she said, a little bleakly. "Or the waterproofing. Or found Cliff a job." She drank carefully out of the side without a chip.

"You don't aim very high, do you," said Molly critically. "Fairy godmothers have the power to produce beautiful castles with their own extensive grounds. Also magic coaches and handsome princes. They don't, that I've ever heard, handle waterproofing. Or Job Creation Schemes." She beamed across at her mother.

But Maureen had not heard a word. Instead she said, urgently, guiltily: "Moll, do you care *very* much about staying in your old attic?"

Yes, said Molly silently. *I do*. "Why?" she said aloud, cautiously.

"It's just that I'd been thinking of getting a lodger—we need the money, Moll. We really do. And then at the class last night, I met this man, another

33

student who has just lost his flat. And I thought, well we *do* have the room...."

Molly avoided her mother's eyes. You mean we have *my* room, she said silently, bitterly. *Not Clifford's room or Sean's room, eh, Mum? We have my room. Don't we?*

"Oh, Molly. Don't look like that. It wouldn't be forever, love. And it costs us such a lot just surviving these days. And you see your room is the natural choice because it's separate from the rest of the house with its own basin and everything." Maureen Gurney reached across the breakfast things to clasp her daughter's hand. "It wouldn't be forever," she repeated.

"When you've got your degree," said Molly hopefully, "you'll be able to get a proper job, won't you?"

Maureen released her hand abruptly and groped for the cigarette pack. "I felt a complete fool last night, Moll. I think my brain has finally turned to mashed potatoes after all these years. It was as if everyone else was talking a foreign language. I'm not up to it, Moll, and that's the truth. If you'd heard the others..." She picked up her mug of tea and drank out of it shakily, and Molly saw to her horror that her mother's eyes had filled with tears.

"I bet they were all just showing off because they were new and scared too and needed to impress everyone else," said Molly fiercely. "And they fooled you. That's all."

Maureen blinked hard over her cigarette. "You think so?"

"No, I don't *think*," growled Molly, scraping back her chair. "I know. Look, Mum, if you have to have my attic for this pompous baldy who talks Ancient Chinese so we can have an extra thirty pounds a week, then have it. I don't care. I'll sleep in Wayne and Chantal's room. But please, Mum, don't give up your course before you've even started it. You're not an idiot, idiot." She touched her mother's hair briefly as she went out. "You're the cleverest person I know."

"Why did you say that?" asked Maureen, following her daughter into the hall.

"What?" Molly shrugged into her outgrown gaberdine. "About you being clever?"

"No. How did you know he was a pompous Ancient Chinese baldy?"

"I don't know."

"It was a surprisingly accurate description, that's all." Maureen was biting her lip and Molly knew she was trying to control the subversive twin sister that stalked about in her head sometimes. In the years of her marriage, that scathing, witty voice had occasionally spoken up too often for Maureen's health. Now she resisted its promptings most of the time. But as Molly was half out of the front door, Maureen said irresistibly: "He looks a bit like an Ancient Chinese, too."

"'Bye, Mum," said Molly with a gathering sense of doom. "I can't wait to see him."

Maureen came to the end of the path in her dressing gown: "I'll phone him then? He can have the room? You don't mind."

If only her mother wouldn't insist that Molly pretended to be happy about it. *I've said it's all right. But she wants me to sing and dance all the way to school about it as well.*

Looking back, her heart lurching suddenly as if she had wandered by mistake into the down lift at Debenhams, Molly simply shook her head to show it was really fine. *It's fine. It's fine. I'll make it fine. It'll just have to be fine.*

Heading homeward once again, after a school day which had been more or less exactly what she had feared it would be, with all the familiar humiliations waiting to pounce on her round every corner, Molly was making positive plans for her move into the little first-floor bedroom.

Its best feature was a deep, old-fashioned window seat, which she decided she would fill glamorously with cushions as soon as she could. And the window itself, though tall and narrow and precariously held up with ancient and rotting sash cords, looked out onto the wild orchard and overgrown cemetery at the back. It would be a good place to dream. It would be even better if Maureen let her take out the two decrepit single beds that took up so much room and bring down her own dear lumpy divan from the attic. These happy thoughts, and the deep relief she felt at not having to deliver any *Bradley Free Echos* for a whole week, accompanied her all the way up the steep cobbled street to her own front door. Which stood open.

"Hello?" called Molly as she threw her coat at its hook, missing by miles as always so that, as always, she had to pick it up from the floor and hang it deliberately and virtuously from the loop under its collar.

The house sounded empty.

She must have popped out to see someone, thought Molly. She doesn't usually leave the front door open though. Neither Cliff nor Sean seemed to be home either. As usual she went straight to the kitchen to get herself some juice.

"I hope you are not dismayed," said a tall, young-looking woman, emerging from the shadows somewhere between the heater and the sink piled with dirty dishes. "I admitted myself into your house in order to wait for you."

Molly took her hand from her pounding chest where it had flown for just a moment. *This is getting to be a habit,* she thought. *People scaring me half out of my skin.* This new visitor was a brilliantly striking figure with jet-black hair that both twisted and coiled elaborately at her nape and still had enough gleaming curls left over to cascade dramatically down her back. Energy snapped off her like sparks. She was in fact very beautiful in a strange and uncomfortable way and so unlike any of Maureen's usual people that Molly stood for a long moment, open-mouthed and stunned, before she recovered herself enough to say, "Oh no, that's okay. Please sit down. My mother shouldn't be long."

The young woman regarded her steadily with clear gray eyes, no, green eyes, decided Molly. But when she walked with a swirl of silk to the old chair and sat down next to the heater, it was immediately obvious that they were actually an amazing violet-blue.

"Are you studying with the Open University?" Molly asked as she put the kettle on, trained since the age of six to put visitors at ease in her mother's kitchen. But she felt disturbed without finally realizing why, by a sherbet sort of fizzing, an invisible singing in the air that she couldn't identify but seemed to remember from somewhere.

The woman laughed, a pleasant laugh from deep in her throat, and her jet hair went flying back over her shoulders like something restlessly alive. "My studying days are well behind me," she said. "Though from time to time I still discover I have much to learn."

"That's what Mum always says," Molly chattered. "She says you go on learning until you die." Not the Open University then. That left the Social Services. Perhaps Mrs. Sutcliffe was on leave, she thought, fishing in the cupboard for biscuits and finding Bourbon creams. As a gesture for the absent Maureen, she carefully arranged them on an old and pretty china plate instead of dumping the whole packet on the table as they normally did.

"I have little time," said the woman suddenly, clasping her hands and then impatiently pushing back the free mass of hair again. "I am not sure how much you have been told. We have not been able to prepare for this as we might have wished, but the event was upon us before we were aware."

She can't be English, thought Molly. I bet she's from somewhere like Chile, a political emigrée or something, and now she's got to work to support herself. If she got really hard up she could always sell some of her jewelry. The woman had raised a slim hand, heavy with many curious silver rings.

"Forgive me," she said urgently. "I must tell you of the child. We do not know fully the extent of the harm that has been done to him. We do not even understand the true nature of it and that troubles us deeply. But he must be kept safe. Without his safety, everything is lost. So if we send him here you must cherish him for us."

Well, that didn't take long, thought Molly. Chantal and Wayne have been gone only a few hours and they want to move another one in. Bang goes my bedroom. Aloud she said, "Does he have night terrors? Don't worry. Maureen knows everything about that kind of thing. He'll be all right here." She held out the plate of biscuits and the woman, almost ceremoniously, took one and held it, examining it curiously without tasting it. Dieting, thought Molly sympathetically, munching away happily herself.

"That is not all," the woman went on, seeming agitated. "You have some understanding, I can see, of the nature of the terror that is locked within this afflicted child. But you see, it may not prove a simple matter to keep him safe. There may be attempts to seize him if it is ever learned—" She broke off. There were sounds of voices and footsteps approaching the back door.

The woman sprang up. "I must leave," she said.

"Don't you want to talk," Molly began, "to my mum..." she ended, not believing her eyes. Surely the woman hadn't opened the door of the pantry and vanished into it?

The kitchen door opened and the front door banged violently as a draft swept through the house. "Oh, *Molly*," exclaimed her mother irritably, coming in laden with bulging suitcases. "You *know* not to leave that front door open. One day the glass is going to shatter and I can't afford to fix it. I've just been helping Mr. Preece fetch some of his things. He's hired a van, but he..." She tailed off, staring at Molly, who in turn was staring wonderingly in through the pantry door at the open stone shelves with all their familiar packets and jars and family clutter. But something was not the same as usual. For one fleeting moment she had, putting her face into the cool gloom, smelled not dried fruit and vanilla and cinnamon, but the green aromatic perfume of forest trees, oak and beech, hazel, hawthorn and rowan, and a sharp tang of sea salt. A fragrance of sea and forests.

"It's not a mouse, is it?" whispered Maureen urgently. "Because if so keep quiet about it and I'll deal with it later." Molly turned just as the cause of Maureen's unnaturally subdued voice came heavily

41

in through the kitchen door carrying a large, ornate and extremely ugly Victorian clock.

"I shall have to put this down," he groaned, and did, there and then, dumping it directly onto the pretty plate Molly had left on the table. It splintered under the impact. Molly saw her mother's face darken and understood who would be receiving the full force of her mother's annoyance, later. Not Mr. Preece, who stood trying to get his breath back and mopping perspiration from his bald forehead. He was a short, pudgy little man with alarmingly bushy eyebrows.

"Mum," she said desperately, "I think a woman from Social Services was here. They've got you another little boy. There's some mystery about him. You know, like a tug-of-love case or something. She was here a minute ago but then she just vanished." She swallowed. She could not tell her mother that the social worker had seemed to vanish into the pantry. Her mother had had to suffer for many years Molly's obsessions with getting into Narnia and would not be amused to think it had started up again.

"Let herself out of the front door, I expect, ninny," said Maureen affectionately. "I thought it was you who'd left it open. Sorry, love. And never mind

42

about the plate," she whispered, moving closer. "It wasn't your fault."

Molly recognized that her mother was trying to make it up to her for losing the attic; also that she was intrigued at the thought of the mystery child.

"Did she say when they'll bring him?" she asked, keeping her voice low. The new member of the household was still waiting, breathing heavily, to learn who would help him lug his possessions up two flights of stairs. Bet I can guess, thought Molly sourly.

"No," she said aloud. "She didn't say very much really. I suppose she just wanted to know if you could cope with him and I said of course. You always cope with everything."

Maureen gave her a humorous look and seemed about to say something, but behind her Henry Preece had suddenly run out of patience and remarked loudly, "I'd better get this lot up to my room then," with such intense resentment in his tone that Molly wanted to giggle outright.

Maureen, her back safely turned to him, mouthed at Molly, "Always. Until now." Then turning to her lodger she said innocently, "I'm sorry, Henry, how rude of me. I haven't introduced you. This is my daughter, Molly. I'm afraid we haven't had time to get all her things out of her room yet, so after

43

we've had a nice cup of tea, perhaps you could help us move her things down, before we take your things up."

Ignoring Molly, Henry Preece stood unmoving for some while, in silence except for his own labored breathing. He seemed to be finding it hard to take in Maureen's words. At last he said: "I've only got the van until seven, you know. It's a favor from a friend. And there's at least one more load to fetch."

"Well then," said Maureen very quietly and pleasantly, "we shall all have to work quite fast in that case, shan't we?"

Inwardly Molly burst into noisy applause. Outwardly she only said, "Would you like me to bring in some of your things?" She watched in fascination as Henry Preece's hairy black brows beetled up into his bald forehead like a pantomime villain's false eyebrows.

"Hmmn," he grunted, still resentful. "I suppose you may as well."

Obedient for her mother's sake, Molly went out to find the van. Yuk, yuk, yuk, she said to herself. What a horrible man. He talks like a grater would talk if a grater talked. I wish we didn't need the thirty pounds a week. And now I'm going to have to share my room with some howling little kid.

Well, at least things can't very well get any worse. What did Gran used to say? When one door shuts, another door closes! Clambering up into the interior of the van, she smiled at the thought of her shrewd, witchy old gran. There was more of her in Maureen than Maureen knew. Then her mouth dropped open. "Things can get worse," she said, staring round, blankly, stunned. "They can even get as bad as this."

The van was full of clocks. It was stacked to the roof with clocks. It was bursting at the seams with clocks.

"Well, now we know at least one reason why his landlady threw him out," she said, nodding to herself. "We have opened our house to a berserk clock freak, Maureen. Maureen Gurney, this is your worst yet."

CHAPTER FOUR

Faded Tapestries

"It's all right," said Maureen much later that night as, exhausted from all the moving, they companionably shared an orange in front of the TV. "Most of them don't work, he says. He says he likes to keep them around to relish the absurdity of mortality."

They had moved Molly's few possessions downstairs into the little back bedroom. At this moment Henry Preece was in her attic, polluting it with his sulky presence: taking possession. Perhaps arranging his clock collection or unfolding harsh, white, varnished-looking sheets to make up his expensive Japanese mattress which he had bought especially, he said, for its lack of comfort. He could have had my divan with the wonky spring that zaps you every time you turn over, for half the price, thought Molly. When he goes I shall have to exorcise that room. Burn branches of flowering sage or juniper in it. Bell, book and candle it.

Sean had gone off to one of the video arcades in Bradley and Clifford, too, had gone roaring off at top speed on some inexplicable errand. Molly sprawled happily on the old sofa and slurped at her half orange. "The absurdity of mortality," she repeated. "That's a translation from the original Mandarin, is it?"

Maureen swatted at her. "You're getting too clever by three quarters, Molly Gurney. Oh, switch this rubbish off, love. It's an insult even to my intelligence. I honestly prefer to think my own small ordinary thoughts than to stuff my head with this silly nonsense."

"'I like best my own vision,'" quoted Molly softly. "That's what the mad old lady said."

"Good for the mad old lady," said Maureen, grinning and lighting up yet again.

If it wasn't for the lines of tiredness around her eyes, Molly thought, Maureen could still be taken for a young girl: her tall slim figure dressed as always in a tatty old sweater and jeans, her unfaded red hair, smooth and silky, not frizzy and bushy like Molly's, bluntly chopped to chin length and worn tucked carelessly behind the ears. She thought that perhaps before she had been married, Maureen might have been beautiful in a wild, shy, prickling kind of way. Certainly not ordinary and oppressed with super gravity like Molly herself.

"Mum," said Molly anxiously as she said nearly every day, "you've got to give up smoking. You really should. If you'd seen the pictures of the lungs they showed us in biology."

Laughing, Maureen put her hands over her ears, miming shutting out whatever lurid details Molly might go into next. "The Indians thought smoke was sacred," she said, as she often did. "Because it rose up in a lovely spiral like the human spirit."

"Well you could always burn joss sticks," suggested Molly. Seeing her daughter's genuinely troubled expression, Maureen sighed and said, as she always did, "I'll just finish this pack, I promise. And then I'll try to give up for good. I know I'm a bad example."

"Wrong. You're a perfect example," said Molly grimly. "I hear you coughing in the mornings, remember." Maureen tossed her half-empty pack mutinously to and fro. Molly began to think she was on the edge of a breakthrough. "Besides," she said trickily, "I bet Mr. Preece doesn't approve of smoking. I unpacked his suitcases on to the pantry shelves. He puts only pure substances into his body. Live Bulgarian yogurt. Sprouting lentils and nettle tea. Organic muesli. He has a special little jug for filtering his drinking water and another little thing for filtering the air in his room. He won't like you flicking ash all around the place, will he?" The rapidly chilling expression in Maureen's eyes told her she had misjudged the situation.

"I'm not sure I'm ready to give up yet, actually," her mother said. "In fact"—she got up and began collecting coffee mugs and orange skins with much more energy than the task required—"I'm suddenly convinced this is the very worst time for me to do it."

She sailed out, leaving Molly wondering how it was that Maureen Gurney, who had been putty in the hands of her sons, her neighbors and almost all living things for the last seventeen or so years, should start her first true rebellion against someone she had only just asked to share her house, and whose money she so desperately needed for her family's survival. Molly privately thought she would not have picked Henry Preece to fight. He seemed the sort of person who might simply steamroller over you without noticing.

Just as her mother, still frosty, came back into

the living room, and Molly, yawning, decided to go up to bed, there was an immense crash at the top of the house, followed by a muffled oath and then, after a drawn-out twangling whirr, as though gargantuan metal springs were uncoiling, came three shrill and somehow appalled cuckoos.

"Well, one of them works," they both said at once, and then they held up little fingers and said "Jinx" and began to laugh helplessly, holding each other up in the doorway, quite weak with silliness. At this moment the front door burst open and Clifford stormed into the hall in his motorbike cowboy outfit.

"You're back early," said Maureen, wiping her eyes. "Is everything all right?"

Without halting his furious ascent, from hallway up the stairs, Clifford bellowed accusingly, "Bloody bike's packed in. What did you *think?*" The door of his room slammed, followed by a deafening blare of sound, followed by a sort of bandaged silence that meant that he had flung himself on his bed with his headset full on.

The front door flew open again and Sean and Vince, arguing at the tops of their booming newly broken voices, bounded heavily up the staircase without a glance at either Molly or Maureen. Just before the cuckoos rang out again, Molly heard

Vince say, "It was my best yet. You didn't see, so you don't know." Sean's door slammed. The cuckoos cuckooed for all they were worth. Sean's computer began to bleat.

"Are you counting to ten?" asked Molly. "You've gone ever so quiet."

"I was just thinking," said Maureen, "that if we crept out now, we could probably be in Australia by Sunday teatime. What do you think?"

"What about your Open University course? And the little boy?" asked Molly. She was secretly shocked to find that Maureen entertained fantasies of walking out on her children. Even overgrown dreadful children who had turned overnight into Urgs and Morgs as Sean and Clifford had done. Perhaps she would really prefer to leave them all behind. Perhaps she had included Molly in her escape plans only because Molly had happened to be there.

"Yes," said her mother, patting Molly absently on the shoulder. "I know. And I promised Mrs. Thorne I'd help at her Rummage Sale for Animal Welfare. Oh hell. I promised Aneela Patel I'd have her little girl. I'm double-booked, Moll."

"I'll have her," said Molly, as she always did. "I don't mind."

"You're an angel," said her mother automatically and without any particular surprise. "I'll see if I can find you a cast-off designer garment at the rummage sale."

"It's actually designer navy-blue gym shorts that I need," said Molly, recalling her humiliating appearance on the school hockey field earlier that day. "Mum, I wish I could have said good-bye to Wayne and Chantal. I really miss them."

"I know. They were nice little kids. Up to bed, Moll. See you in the morning." Maureen had turned her head supercasually away to peer at the clock on the mantelpiece. But Molly was not deceived. She didn't need to see her mother's tears. They had already sprung hotly to her own eyes in sympathy.

Molly doesn't know if she is dreaming or waking. First the voices begin: murmurings, whisperings and suppressed gigglings in passages of echoing stone. A snatch of song. Children's voices. Everything is shadowy, the light so dim that shapes loom out at her like ghosts and then dissolve. She can hear a small child crying and another older child quieting it in a carrying, rather bossy voice.

"But where's she gone, Minna?" wails the little one.

And someone, presumably Minna, hisses: "It's a secret and we're not supposed to know of it. Won't you hush?"

"But I want Mama now," persists the little one, its voice rising dangerously.

He'll be screaming his head off in a minute, thinks

Molly. But clearly Minna knows a thing or two. "Come down to the kitchen with me and I'll make Nan give you some of the sugar plums she bought as a fairing," she coaxes, her voice softer than kittens. "Be a good boy, Eddie. Soon she will come home again, and till then Orlando and I will take turns to tell you stories."

"Did I say I would?" interrupts another voice, a boy's, drawling, superior.

"Why certainly he will," flashes Minna, her sweet kitten voice unexpectedly unsheathing claws. "For if he does not, someone must tell Papa how it was the gargoyle face came to be carved into the door of the tutor's room when he was away visiting his mother."

Molly tosses, turns. She mutters: "I wish I could see properly." And as if a switch is thrown, the fog before her eyes swirls, clean, is whisked away. But she is frustrated to find she is now presented with an entirely strange scene.

She is looking at a fire of driftwood that burns brightly on an open hearth. She has not the least idea where she is, yet she is suddenly overwhelmed with a sense of homecoming so powerful and absolute that it makes her eyes sting. The room is octagonal, high-ceilinged, many-windowed and filled with the soft fret and dazzle of the sea. Suspended in the windows, hanging from crossbeams, stored on shelves and in bowls and baskets everywhere, are beautiful crystals of every imag-

inable shape, size and color. Perhaps it's the crystals that give the room its dazzling magical quality. She feels as if she is wrapped round with rainbows or peacefully drowning under a silent sunlit ocean. On each of the walls between the windows, old gigantic tapestries hang from ceiling to floor. Some natural alchemy of salt sea air, the pure brilliancy of the light and the passing years have weathered and faded the once-rich colors of these woven pictures unevenly to bleached-out duns, grays, lavenders. Almost to silver in places. And it seems to Molly that the tapestries have been arranged in this room for the specific purpose of telling a story and that this is one of the reasons she is here. Only she is not alone.

Leaning his elbows on a large plain wooden table amongst a litter of maps, plans and unfamiliar instruments that make Molly think uncomfortably of mathematics, is a man with a narrow, pouncing kind of face like a hunting hawk, and hair that is streaked black and silver. His hands are large and square-fingered like a potter's, and he is weighting the corners of one of the charts with little lumps of raw crystal to stop it curling over. She can even read the strange flowery calligraphy, in ink as faded as the tapestries, that flows across the yellowing surface of the shoreline and the sea: "Old Hallowes—The Place of the Heartstone—Launde."

Molly shivers. Danger crackles through and around

this man like high-voltage electricity. Something tells her he has waited and watched in this magic room too long. What his work might be she cannot imagine, but she knows he is searching for something. The room seems to be used partly as a study or workroom and partly as some kind of observatory. There is a great clumsy telescope that points upward into the glossy dome of the tower. She is drawn back to the tapestries.

But before she can turn her attention properly to the one nearest her, a woman enters the room and stands uncertainly, awkwardly, as if she might after all decide to bolt back through the door. Her face is hidden in the shadow of a richly furred hood, but Molly feels the churning of her painful emotions as if they sprang from her own body: a stormy withdrawn woman, almost ill with grief. When she speaks at last, her tone is low-pitched, beautiful, but her words are bitter.

"I come here in secret not because I trust you, for now I trust no one, but because you are my last hope. I come to you in shame like a woman driven to warlocks to buy a love potion to keep everything she holds dear. It is you and your dark arts or my child's death—or worse than death. And I will not let the Magus have him. I will not let him be taken to that place. Well—will you help me? I would bring you gold and silver but I know you would scorn it." She is breathing fast—she almost stretches out her hands to beseech the hawk-

faced man and Molly sees how much they tremble. Then, as if furious and disgusted at her own weakness, she thrusts her shaking hands behind her back.

"The Kingdom of Launde has fallen into evil times indeed," says the man, "when the Lord and the Lady ask the unbelonging for gifts. Next I will hear that the world is upside down and the poacher of the Lord's deer is turned magistrate and the beggars at your gate shall rule the Treasury." He rises from the table and before Molly's disbelieving eyes shimmers briefly into the bent and ancient figure of a beggar in filthy rags. "Alms," he whines. "Alms." Then he is himself: a dangerously calm presence, flickering with some barely suppressed lightning. "But I have here the piece of silver your son, Merlin, gave to me. So we will not say 'gift' since the Lord and Lady have paid their fee already."

If the Lady recalls an incident with a beggar she gives no sign of it but replies angrily, "Not the Lord and the Lady. The Lady alone is asking. If my Lord Gilbert knew what I know, would I have come alone and in peril to your tower? I grew up with the teachings of the women of my household and they taught me what you are, you Three. I know the old stories so many have forgotten, Keeper of Launde. You need not play your games with me. Did you think I never heard the old Riddle? Do you think I have never heard of the Three who Watch and Wait and Remember?" Her *gaze wanders distractedly now around the room, taking in the crystals that burn with their lovely colored fires like Northern Lights, then she stares at her feet. "I wish you could find what they say you seek," she says, almost softly. "I wish those old legends had some grain of truth and Launde could become again what it once was." Then she lifts her head, jutting her chin, her eyes guarded and suspicious once more. "Myself, I believe only what I can see, touch and give a name to, and I know he has brought this evil on me. His line is evil. It was always so. He titles himself Magus. But I say Monster or Devil."*

"We cannot touch the stars, Lady Agnes. Sometimes without our instruments we may not even see them, yet we know they are there—and so believe me when I tell you there are stars within and they are as mysterious and, like the stars without, they have their eclipses and conjunctions, their harmonies and disharmonies." He is looking piercingly at the Lady as though willing her to understand something beyond his words. Idly, Molly notices a strange toy pushed into a dusty corner of a shelf: Its threads are knotted and entangled, clotted with the dust of centuries. Its little crystal planets, stars, moons dangle awkwardly, off balance where they should be held precisely in their stately dance around a central sun. She has a sudden possessive impulse. How nice it would look, mended and spruced up so that the

dulled and grimy crystal spheres danced and bowed once again, endlessly taking in and giving out light. It would look lovely hanging in my window, she thinks.

But the Lady is still quarrelsome. "You fling out words like moonshine and sea mist only to blind and bewilder me, Keeper. Men ever like to impress women with their wisdom." She is pacing agitatedly. "You know why I have come. If I were not a woman, I would—but it is not fit work for me, so I have come to ask you to use your powers to prevent the Magus. They say that in your search you have acquired powers beyond even his imagining. If you would, you could destroy him and end this suffering—in our lifetime at least."

The Keeper gazes at her, his expression sphinxlike. "I have another rule of moonshine and sea mist, Lady, despise it if you will. I have learned that there are worlds in which our presences shine like stars and worlds where what appear on earth to us as stars manifest as other orders of beings about their own lives and lessons. And so within the mysterious universe of your own body may there not also be infinitesimal beings, sentient as yourself, to whom your veins are rushing rivers, whose mountain ranges are your common bones? To these beings might not your rages shake the ground like earthquakes, your griefs appear as tidal waves? Might they not struggle amongst themselves to find the flawed one, the cursed one who has brought down on them all

58

their woes? So he be punished and they released from suffering? Yet, still there would be earthquakes, tidal waves, in which these beings have played their own part unaware—Lady Agnes, can you tell me why we have lost the wit and courage to frame even such questions each tiny child asks as soon as it can utter? When we were all born to undertake this work, why must so many, like the Magus, turn all art and power inward to destruction?"

"Harmonies, disharmonies within and without! Keeper, these are either products of faulty digestion or else fireside philosophies more fitting for another time," says the Lady angrily. She throws back her hood. Red-gold hair tumbles down her back. Blue crystal drops like tears flash fire from the lobes of her ears. "I am not so weak and powerless as you might suppose. I am the Lady of the Castle of the Forests, one of the Seven Households. You live on in secret in this wild place only by women's superstitious fears and your own dissembling. Therefore I charge you to help me!" She draws herself up, tall and proud, and around her a shimmer of power begins to form like a lit mist, full of intriguing little flares and detonations of brilliantly intense color. Molly holds her breath.

The hawk-faced man laughs outright. "What a kingdom of dabbling little conjurers we have become," he says. "Three a brass penny. Round every corner and in every ditch and castle, too, it seems." With calm indifference he turns his back on her to replace a worn volume on a shelf.

The woman bites at her lip, the cloud of power ebbing slowly in a sunset glow. "I come to beg and plead but even that is not enough to salve your rascal's bitterness," she says at last, though Molly thinks she hasn't done a great deal of begging and pleading. "Perhaps there is no hope after all. Perhaps the Keepers have spent too long grubbing in hedges, beachcombing the shores for lost knowledge. Perhaps dreaming of lost perfection and ancient riddles, they have forgot what they most need to remember: human pain and human love. I love my little son. But he is already lost if you deny me. And you give me not even the courtesy of reply."

The hawk-faced man pushes his hands roughly back through his hair. Now there is something in his face that was not there before. When he speaks it is with a strange, half-reluctant tenderness. "I am sorry, Lady, but you have understood none of the old stories that have come down to you, ragged and threadbare with telling, if you believed the Keepers would use their hard-worn power to take a life, even such a life as you may loathe, and to save an innocent. When we so use our powers against another, we destroy ourselves. You have appealed? There is no hope of mercy?"

She looks away. "You know there is not. We expect

his men at any moment. For all I know, even now they batter at the castle gate." She staggers slightly, recovers and sternly grips her own elbows with whitening hands, forcing her grief under control. "My noble Lord locks himself in his chamber, blaming me for all, speaking to no one. And all the fools about me say" (she mimics savagely): "'Oh, Lady, it is written in the stars!' As if they had the dulled obedient minds of cattle that file to the dairy to be milked. My poor little ones are braver and wiser than any of them—but I cannot, I will not explain the poisoned history of this foul curse. What they hear whispered by night, though, I know not...." Unable to speak for a long while, as though sleepwalking, she moves haltingly to stand before one of the tapestries, staring at it, but blindly. Then she says despairingly, "Even the fountains in our courtyard run dry, as though the very source of life itself has turned upon us. Does it speak of this in your old prophecies, Keeper? Is this the downfall for which the Keepers wait?"

"You do not submit," he says drily, "to what is written in the start?"

"A little child," she says, shaking her head. "Not four years old. A babe. How is it possible he should be cursed? I cannot sleep, Keeper. I cannot eat. I have no rest knowing what they will—" She breaks off and then abruptly says in a startled tone, "Why, here are the lovers." For the first time, she really looks at the tapestry before her. "This is Dominis as they sing of him in our house, golden-haired as a lion. He sings and plays to Cassia. Her hair is black as a raven's in the song, but time and salt have silvered it. Time deals harshest with women. They say it was with his music he won her. But the Law forbade their betrothal; isn't that how the old songs go, Keeper?" She is moving from one tapestry to the next, her head tilted back like an attentive child's, almost as though she can hear the music of old sad lost songs and is drawn into a strange, formal, circling dance half against her will. All the time she fiercely grips her own elbows. "And so here they die in each other's arms. And when the old Magus of those days, Cassia's father, heard of her death, he howled out a curse so terrible that the Heartstone, the magical source of all our good, split into seven shards as though lightning-struck. And since that day, Launde ceased to be great and prosperous, the sweet forest kingdom. And so they say our woes began."

"Some tell the story so," agrees the Keeper. "But once I heard another tale, Lady, which told how the Heartstone loved and sensed and suffered for all the kingdom's living things, as would a human heart, and when such things as dynasties and affairs of state were put before two children and their natural happiness, the Mother Crystal shattered under the weight of its own grief. Sometimes I have wondered if we will ever find the lost shard of the Heartstone, for all our arts, until we learn to love our children as we ought."

"Do you speak to me of love, Keeper? That is because you are not a woman. Love weakens all our sex or else I would not be here. A steady burning fuse of hatred is what all men use to defeat their enemies." She is motionless again, standing now before the final tapestry. "The centuries have not made alteration, Keeper," she says, her voice low but charged with loathing. "This day he still looks so, as though he lived again, as though he rose again to curse us." Molly follows her gaze and shudders at the figure of the Magus, standing over the body of his beautiful dead daughter, his head lifted like a wolf howling its pain. She can't tell if her horror is her own foreboding or the terrible contagious dread of Lady Agnes.

"We shall take your babe and hide him," says the Keeper, seeming to look idly out of the window. "We shall hide him as carefully as it may be done. Now go and take care you are not seen. When the time comes, if we have chosen his guardian well . . . you may yet hold him in your arms again."

"But better by far to lose him," she bursts out, "to safe and loving arms forever, than to the living death they plot for him in Launde." She is concealed within *the folds of her cloak once more. She lifts her hand in an awkward gesture to the face Molly can no longer see, as if to scrub away any traces of tears that might betray her. Without another word she leaves.*

CHAPTER FIVE

The Third Visitor

Saturday was sunny: a cool, springlike day. When Molly hung the sheets out on the line and gazed up at the almost cloudless sky, she felt herself falling upward into limitless blue. Even with her feet sensibly on the earth she could see for miles today. Everything had clear, sharp edges, like glass.

Henry Preece went off early to an auction at a country house on the outskirts of Bradley.

"Guess what he'll come back with," said Molly wickedly.

But Maureen seemed to have forgotten her evening of subversion and said reprovingly, "He's a very lonely man, Molly. Imagine a grown man living in a series of dismal rented rooms with only a collection of broken old clocks for company. It's really very sad."

You thought it was very funny last night, thought Molly. But all she said was, "What does he do? Where does he actually work?"

"Council Offices," said Maureen. "I think. Something to do with taxes, I have a nasty feeling."

Clifford got up at lunchtime and demanded a huge fried breakfast, which Maureen, as usual, tolerantly cooked, though she had one eye nervously on the clock because of the rummage sale. Then he went outside and began to take his motorbike apart all over the Gurneys' small backyard. Molly took him out a mug of tea, took the sheets off the line as a precaution against motorbike oil and said rashly, "Are you sure you know how to put it back together again?"

But he seemed in a better mood today: She had actually heard him whistling in the bathroom, and all he said was, "Nothing to it. Garages are daylight robbery." And went back to his tinkering.

"Right, I'm off," said Maureen, grabbing her old fawn raincoat from the hook in the hall. "Say hello to Aneela for me."

"I'll take Shushi to the park," said Molly. "Try to remember the designer clothes."

Molly and Shushi spent a pleasant hour or so in the park, feeding ducks and swinging on swings, and then they ambled home again for orange juice and biscuits, comfortable in each other's company. Three-year-old Shushi mainly spoke Gujarati but she knew how to make herself understood in essential matters like biscuits. They beamed at each other across the table in the Gurneys' kitchen.

Then Shushi said, in her deliberately beguiling tones, her melting dark eyes insistently appealing from under her glossy black fringe: "You get puppets, Molly. You *get* them."

Molly raised an eyebrow. "Magic word?" she said sternly.

"Pleece."

Cheerfully, Molly went upstairs to find the box of wooden puppets she had loved herself when she was small. As well as the puppets themselves there was a small plywood theater with a choice of two painted scenes: "Inside the Castle" and "In the Forest." The cast included a prince and princess, a peasant boy and girl, a witch and a trickster.

When she was small she had spent hours concocting dramas out of her favorite fairy tales. The trouble was that however carefully Molly laid them in their box, the puppets had always mysteriously-retangled their strings when she took them out again.

Coming downstairs, her arms full, Molly heard Shushi's imperious small voice explaining something to someone. She hesitated a second before she went into the kitchen. There was a tingling feeling in the air that she was coming to recognize and now something was chiming silently inside her in answer. *I am the First Visitor. There will be Three in all.*

Something is happening, thought Molly. I've been pretending it isn't. I've been pretending it's just ordinary, but if I go in the kitchen now, I shan't be able to pretend anymore. Then the strange tingling vanished and she walked stoutly in through the kitchen door, just as Shushi said something excitedly in Gujarati, pointing and laughing at the pantry door, and the visitor, also laughing, said something Molly did not catch in reply.

"Can I help you?" asked Molly politely, setting down her boxes on the table. "Wait, Shushi, we've got to untangle them first."

"I am hoping that you can help me," agreed the man. It was hard to tell how old he was. Molly was thrown off-balance by an overwhelming awareness of having seen him before, but she could not imagine where. Her main impression was of an almost dangerous, electric intelligence and restlessness, and he seemed very tall in the Gurneys' shabby kitchen. His face reminded her of a fierce bird's—a hawk's, she thought. He was dressed in a white shirt with rather impractical full sleeves, and all his other garments seemed worn and dark and uncared for. He looked like the picture of Hamlet she had seen in an old school Shakespeare of her mother's, except that he was clearly not so sorry for himself as Hamlet had looked, and he had rather shaggy hair that was streaked dramatically black and silver.

"You don't want to see my mother," Molly stated flatly. He shook his head silently, gazing at her with eyes that shifted color: green, gray, violet.

"And if I offer you food or drink, you'll accept it very politely but you won't eat or drink," she said almost accusingly. Shushi looked in a puzzled way from one to the other.

"Why have you come?" Molly asked. She suddenly felt very brave. She felt as if someone else much older, not Molly Gurney, was speaking. "Please do sit down," she added. And sat down coolly herself and got on with untangling the peasant girl.

The hawk-faced man sat down, and as he did so Molly caught out of the corner of her eye once again that shivering, hardly visible, forked-lightning effect. The tingling was back in the room, her own inner chiming tumultuous. To keep herself steady she breathed slowly.

"We are sorry this has all taken so long," he said

courteously, "but there have been so many other elements to consider. It is the first experiment of this kind we have undertaken, you see. But your application was breathtakingly powerful in its timing, from our point of view, and most impressive."

Molly stiffened at what she took to be mockery. What was he talking about? She hadn't applied for anything. She gave him a puzzled, guarded glance, saw what he held out, smiling, to her and gasped.

"My advertisement! How—?"

In his hand was her own torn and forgotten piece of paper, fished out of the dresser drawer, imprinted with her own foolish longings and imaginings and last seen by her charring into a blackened ruin. Yet it was the same paper: perhaps a little scorched, but miraculously whole, her own uneven handwriting instantly recognizable. "QUESTS UNDERT..." she could read. "...MENTS BROKEN..."

"I don't understand," she said suspiciously. "How have you done that? Is it a trick?"

"You could describe it thus," agreed her visitor, folding up the piece of paper and putting it into an inner pocket.

Shushi was getting impatient. "Puppets, Molly," she said, tugging.

"I've got to get the tangles out of the strings," said poor Molly, her fingers struggling helplessly because of the utterly confused state of her mind. Had this man come in answer to her unsent *advertisement*? It was impossible. She wouldn't believe it.

"What some men call 'spells' others call simply 'Words of Power,'" said the hawk-faced stranger softly, as though answering her thoughts. "Any words may take wing when the heart yearns to soar beyond its bounds. A pretty toy," he added in a louder voice. "I may be able to help." He leaned forward and blew gently onto the heap of puppets. Shushi giggled, but he held up first the prince in his doublet and hose and then the witch in her drab black to show her that all the knots and snarls had now vanished. "Now she will dance for you," he said, gently dancing the witch in front of her.

"No," said Shushi, shrinking back in dread. "Bad witch."

"You are wrong," said the stranger reprovingly. "She is but an old wise woman who understands the magic of the earth. If you listen carefully, perhaps she will tell you one of her secrets."

Timid, but responsive to his air of authority, Shushi crept closer and put her ear to the witch puppet as if listening. A private smile spread slowly over her face and she said something soft and apologetic in Gujarati.

"Has she forgiven you for your harsh words?"

asked the hawk-faced man, smiling. Shyly, Shushi nodded her glossy head. "I knew she would. Like the earth itself she is forgiving."

"She understood you!" cried Molly. "She's understood everything you've said to her. But she hardly knows any English."

But the stranger, turning his attention from Shushi, had become silent, attentive, as though listening with intense concentration to something a long way off. Then, almost ceremoniously, he said: "Molly Gurney, could you tell me if you have noticed any change in yourself since three nights past?"

"You mean the sort of singing," said Molly, the words speaking themselves as if someone else were answering, someone who understood the deeper purposes of his words. "Like something singing from inside my bones. I think I've always had it, but just lately it keeps happening all the time."

"Yes," he said, seeming pleased. "Yes. Now there is no doubt that you are the guardian we are seeking. Long ago I was told that the *unbelonging* are seeded like the starry dandelion throughout all the worlds and that it is possible for us to meet and know each other at once. In dreams we meet and speak and exchange mysteries. In some worlds we more easily forget our natures.... But you have offered yourself to us for the work.... You have

72

been told what will be asked of you? The dangers?"

"There is a child," said Molly haltingly. The tingling in the air was becoming unbearable. It was hard to breathe.

"And you will cherish him for so long as need be. He will be brought to you at a fitting hour," began the stranger, rising from his chair, but just as Molly, with a flash of rebellion, was going to inquire, "Fitting for you or for us did you mean?" Shushi tripped over the rag rug, fell sprawling and struck her head on a corner of the table with a piercing wail of real distress. Molly flew to her and gathered her up in her arms, making soothing noises. The stranger stood, forgotten, watching her, smiling almost sadly. Then he turned and was gone. When Shushi had stopped crying, the pantry door was swinging gently on its hinges and the hawk-faced man was nowhere to be seen.

At this point, for just one uncomfortable moment, there were two separate and distinct Mollys in the kitchen. The one who grew and reached out and shone and the one who shrank like a boiled sweater.

"Now I know it will happen," said the first Molly inside herself, her bones positively orchestral. "There will be Three in All. That was the Third one.

They tested me and now they've chosen me. And now it will happen."

"Now this is getting ridiculous," said the second Molly. "Shushi, I think I'm going mad." She carried the tearstained, hiccupping little girl over to the pantry and, feeling a complete fool, peered into its cool gloom. Now there was only one of her, confused, almost frightened and on the edge of tears herself.

"The first time it was sand with bits of jewel stuff in it," she said to herself. "The second time it smelled like forests after the rain, with a whiff of sea salt. But this time"—she sniffed hard—"it's *all* seashore. Salt and seaweed, Shushi. Just like Robin Hood Bay. But you know and I know that Bradley is about a hundred miles away from the sea."

Not the other house. The other house isn't a hundred miles from the sea. If you climbed into that tall white tower you could see and hear the waves coming in. You could hear the gulls cry. You could see over the forest. But what else? What else could you see?

But the other house was a sort of day dream, not real like strange visitors to her home on Vine Street, doing conjuring tricks with lightning effects and burned notes and tangled string. And even those things weren't real in the same way that everyday life on Vine Street was real.

"Biscuit?" said Shushi hopefully, still shuddering slightly. "Biscuit and juice?"

Molly found antiseptic cream for Shushi's bumped head and a biscuit to cheer her up, but she couldn't put her heart into the stories she told her, or the games she played with her as they waited for Aneela Patel to come and pick her up. Molly was inwardly reeling with several conflicting versions of the events of the last three days. And none of them made the usual kind of sense.

CHAPTER SIX

"Cherish Mee"

Several days passed and Molly's life returned to normal. She had no more strange visitors. Perhaps I just sort of pretended it all to make things seem less boring, she thought. Well, probably to make *me* seem less boring. When she remembered how sorry she had been for herself the night of the storm, she felt ashamed.

Cliff put his motorbike back together with apparent success. The lovely spring weather lingered. To the disgust and resentment of the resident family cat, a torn-eared ginger bruiser called Perkins, Maureen acquired two tiny kittens from a disreputable neighbor who swore on his mother's life that he had pulled them out of the river. Molly privately suspected he was more likely to have put them in than to pull them out. She also doubted if they could have survived even a mouthful of the local river water, which ran past several evil-smelling factories before it wound up in their part of Bradley. But they were rather nice kittens, glossy, rippling, silken black all over like witches' cats with wide and wondering blue eyes; Licorice and Lucifer their official names. In practice you just called "Kittens!" into the air, and both kittens came bounding and squeaking like a single entity to be fed.

The guinea pig recovered and Molly found it a job as a school guinea pig in the school animal house, where it later efficiently produced several litters of patchwork piglets. Henry Preece took to growing moldering moss on layers of damp white lint on the Gurneys' kitchen windowsill: extraordinarily nutritious in wholemeal sandwiches, he said. Henry Preece and Molly disliked each other intensely from the beginning. For her mother's sake, Molly kept her enmity covert and silent. Henry Preece, on the other hand, exercised his sullen belligerence wherever and whenever their paths crossed. He was, as she had known as soon as she set eyes on him, a man who did push-ups in a string vest and pajama trousers first thing in the morning: a man who talked at you, not to you. A man with the sense of humor of a newt. As the days went by he spent more of his time lecturing Maureen on how to run her household and complete her Open University assignments than on winding his clocks upstairs. But Maureen so far had managed to remain polite, tolerant, even vaguely friendly. And the singing in Molly's bones died down as if it had never been.

I am meant to be an ordinary person, she told herself as she pushed the last few *Echos* through the last few letter boxes on her round. Ordinary is written all over me, and probably all through me, too, like seaside rock. If I can just get on with the business of being ordinary, everything will be all right. I've got an ordinary face and ordinary great big clumping feet and I shall leave school and get an ordinary job as an ordinary children's nurse or something. Or more likely, be on the ordinary dole. Oh no! One left over again.

Deliberately she looked away from Albert Villas as she walked back home. *Ordinary*, she repeated firmly. But as she turned up Vine Street, she couldn't resist opening the extra *Echo* and turning to the stars to see what Tamara had cooked up for her this week.

"Trust yourself," said Tamara mysteriously. *"You*

*understand better than you think you do. In the days
to come you will need all your resources.*"

"You are a survivor," intoned Molly hollowly, flapping her paper like ghostly wings as she climbed back up Vine Street.

"But you don't know it yet. Ah, what next." She turned to the next birthday and froze. "*Someone may be entrusted to your care. Even your love may not save him unless you are strong. But more than you can imagine depends on you now.*"

On the instant, the air began to tingle, and deep in the marrow of her ordinary down-to-earth bones, Molly felt the reawakening of her mysterious inner song. And as she did, she realized that the self she had been since the singing had stopped was appallingly less than her real self, less real, less alive. But until it returned, her secret song, she had not known, had not understood. *It comes from the new me, the song, from the me I'm growing into. And when I get home the child will be there.*

She began to run the last few hundred meters up the hill in an agony of expectation. Suppose the child were not there. Suppose he *were!* How would she ever explain it to Maureen? What could she do if he really was in danger? Must she take care of him forever, or would the visitors come back for him when the danger, whatever it was, was over?

Whyever hadn't she asked these questions while she had the chance? And why was she so sure that a few obscurely worded predictions in the stars column of a stupid small-town trade paper were meant just for her?

She burst in at the back door to find the kitchen empty. Maureen's books and papers were spread all over the table, so she couldn't have gone far. Licorice and Lucifer, twisted together in a furry plait in the ironing basket, blinked sleepy yellow slits at her and yawned enormously.

"Okay," said Molly to them. "This is silly, but I have to do it. Just don't ask why." She flung open the pantry door. Empty. "I told you it was silly," said Molly.

Then she heard Maureen's voice calling in an unusually soft, hushed tone from upstairs. "That you, Moll? Come up a minute, will you? Come here."

"Where's here?" Molly hissed back from the hall.

"Your room. You won't believe this. I can't believe it myself."

Her heart thudding, Molly went softly up the stairs to the little back bedroom. Maureen was sitting on the edge of the spare bed. Beside her, making a small, scarcely breathing mound under the quilt, was a sleeping child.

Molly drew closer, hardly breathing herself. The

tingling in the air around her was so violent she was sure Maureen must notice it.

"He looks exhausted," she whispered. "And so unhappy. And pale."

Maureen's face was grim. "Can you believe how I found him? I know the country's got all these cuts and everything, but he'd just been *dumped* here. I found him asleep on that pile of old velvet curtains I brought back from the rummage sale. Skinny, pale little mite, all over bruises, and all he had on was this thin little shirt, just like one of those old-fashioned nightshirts. It's beautiful material, all hand-sewn ivory silk, look. But who'd want to bother nowadays when you can get such lovely things in Mothercare?" She paused for breath.

"His hair is so *long*," said Molly softly. The little boy's hair drifted back over the white pillow in tangling tendrils of pale gold, like honeysuckle. "And he has an earring," she said, startled. In one earlobe a hole had been pierced and a jeweled stud was fastened in it. The jewel winked like a small star, from rose to lavender to pure clear diamond white.

"It changes color," said Maureen. "With the light. I've been looking at it. It's much too big and heavy for a little boy, isn't it?"

"Are you sure he's all right?" asked Molly. "He's

81

sleeping so deeply." An enchanted sleep, she thought. He's in an enchanted sleep. The singing in her bones recognized it and rose half an octave.

"Yes. He's quite warm and he's breathing normally," said Maureen. "But *who* is he, that's what I want to know. And why was he dumped here without any explanation, without any clothes—without anything to identify him? You wait till I ring up Social Services. I shall give them a piece of my mind. I know they think I'm anyone's mug to take on everyone's bundle of trouble any time of day or night, but this is the limit. It's just cruel to leave a child like this without introducing him to us first. What's he going to think when he wakes up amongst strangers?"

Molly shook her head. "Among Gurneys," she corrected. "I'll go and make us a cup of tea, Mum. We'll sort this out later."

Oh help, help, help! she thought, flying down the stairs. I'm a hundred percent sure he hasn't any connection at all with Social Services. What shall I say when she finds out? What shall I do?

It felt strange to be making tea. Here she was, caught in a web of something she could only describe to herself with embarrassment as magic. Yet she was waiting for the kettle to boil and wishing Sean and Vince hadn't pinched the last of the Bourbon creams. The kettle was taking ages. She paced and paced and then, oddly compelled, went again to the pantry, turned the door handle and walked in. Everything was normal. Boxes of Weetabix; packets of sugar; half a huge apple pie in which she could smell the cloves; Henry Preece's organically grown muesli. She looked up. Cobwebs: and a moth, folded into itself like a small scrap of muslin. Nothing, she told herself. Nothing. Then, backing out of the pantry, her foot collided with a soft something. She bent down. On the tiled floor was a cloth bundle, tied in a complex knot.

It's his. I know it is.

The kettle began to scream. She took the bundle into the kitchen and made the tea, her hands trembling with excitement.

"I thought I'd leave him," said Maureen, coming in. "We'll hear him if he wakes and I don't think he'll be waking for a while, yet. Poor little scrap. Looks as if he's been dragged halfway round the world and back—those shadows under his eyes. I've seen some sad and hurt children in my time but this one—What is it, love?" Molly was holding out the bundle to her.

"I've found something. I think it's his."

Maureen laid it on the table and with deft and patient fingers puzzled out and finally unfastened the knot. The cloth fell open. "His worldly goods," she said wryly, "I presume."

In a neatly pressed and folded pile were a small handsewn shirt of rose-colored silk and a waistcoat of dove-gray velvet, lined with what might be lambswool. To match the waistcoat were some kind of trousers. There were two pairs of soft knitted socks, moss green, rather shapeless, that looked as if they were intended to be fastened with yarn ties, and a pair of small soft leather boots.

"Someone's sent the contents of his dressing-up box by mistake," said Maureen. "Whoever could have provided a child with such peculiar clothes?"

"I love them," said Molly, stroking the beautiful little shirt. "I think they're really pretty." She lifted up the waistcoat to look at it closely. "There's something in the pocket. It's a little comb, look, wrapped in some kind of paper."

Maureen took the comb from her, examining it curiously. "What lovely craftsmanship," she said. "Bone, is it? Or ivory. Carved with tiny leaves and flowers."

The paper had fluttered to the floor. Molly picked it up, wondering if it would be fine and handmade like everything else. It was soft and silken to the touch and dotted with little patches of unevenness, as if the seeds and fibers of some plant had been incorporated into it. Then—"Something's written on it!" she yelled. "Look."

"I'm not deaf," Maureen complained. "You read it. I haven't got my specs."

"It's just like old-fashioned writing," said Molly. "It's not very easy to read.

"'I am Floris,'" she read. "'Take good Care that you telle No manne I am lodged with you for there be Enemies aboute. Bee not Annoy'd with mee that I cannot Speake. Myne Enemies have laid a Spelle on mee since my Birthe. I understand welle enow. Bee Assur'd that in Tyme, Frendes wille come to Beare me to mine owne House. For Nowe I am Indebted to your Charitie. Cherish mee.' Cherish me," she whispered.

"Floris!" said Maureen indignantly. "Why didn't they call him Parsifal and be done with it! He's obviously been living with some really disturbed people. Do you think it's one of those religious sects? That could explain the weird language and the persecution complex. It sounds vaguely biblical, doesn't it? Where are the cigarettes? I'm gasping. It's no use you hiding them, Moll. This is not the moment to wean me off the weed."

"You're assuming," said Molly, handing the pack over grudgingly, "that the weird people who treated him badly are the same people as the ones who wrote the note and brought him here. But the message says they want us to cherish him. They want us to keep him safe. They trust us to look after him. I mean, maybe someone really does want to harm him. Just because we can't understand what's going on, doesn't mean it isn't serious. And he's mute, it says. But not deaf. He can understand."

"Yes, but that could be just because he's so disturbed or frightened. I mean, Moll. All that rubbish about *spells*."

"I know," sighed Molly hypocritically. At the same time thinking: What have you let me in for, people from out of the pantry? An enchanted child from a different time or world or dimension or something. And I'm supposed to keep him safe. But who am I keeping him safe from, exactly? How will I recognize "the Enemy" when I see him or her? Or *them*, she thought, with a spasm of fear. And if they turn out to be the kind of enemies that chuck spells about when they get angry, whatever use will I be? And what do I do when I'm at school?

"Oh dear," said Maureen crossly. "Everyone will be back in a minute and I haven't even thought about supper. I was going to make a lovely pie but there isn't time now. I'll have to be ever so inspired with leftovers."

"Well you needn't worry about Henry," said

Molly. "He can have his nutritious mold on toast. The rest of us can have eggs and french fries. I'll do the spuds. You listen out for Floris in case he's woken up and feels lonely."

But Floris slept motionless throughout the evening. Once when Molly crept in to check on him, she found the kittens had sneaked onto the end of his bed. Each opened a wary slit of eye to see if Molly was going to throw them out and then, rippling and purring under her stroking hand, settled back to sleep again.

"Company for you," she murmured. "I wonder what you're dreaming. Hope it's nice. Still, if you stay like this all the time, I shan't have too much trouble keeping you out of mischief, shall I?"

CHAPTER SEVEN

Floris Gurney

Several times in the night, Molly half woke and raised herself up on her elbow to peer across at the still-motionless form of the sleeping child. There was something eerie about his sleep. It might look natural, but then perhaps Sleeping Beauty had looked and seemed natural enough: warm to the touch, her breathing deep and regular. But she hadn't woken for a hundred years. Or was it a thousand? Sighing, disturbed but dreadfully tired, Molly plunged back again and again into her own troubled dreams.

She was hacking desperately through thickets of bramble to reach him when sunlight struck her full between the eyes, through the gap where her skimpy curtains didn't quite meet, and she sat up shaken. The dial on her alarm clock told her it was 9:30. She had overslept. And Floris's bed was empty.

Panic seized her. She threw back her bedcovers frantically and then let out a huge, noisy sigh of relief, not bothering after all to get to her feet.

Floris was sitting on the floor, solemnly examining the wooden puppets. When he saw Molly watching him, he showed no surprise, but gazed back at her with large, beautiful eyes the color of wild violets, and slowly smiled. Then he scrambled to his feet in his little silk nightshirt, ran to her, and to her utter astonishment threw his thin arms around her neck. She could feel his heart beating.

"Well, hello little rabbit," she said shakily. "You woke up after all. Let me look at you properly." He stood back obediently, his pale-gold hair a wild nimbus around his small pointed pale face.

"Maureen said you were badly bruised all over," she said, surprised. "But I can't see a mark on you. You must heal ever so quickly. Have you been awake long?" He smiled and shook his head no.

"Do you know who I am? My name's Molly." He nodded gravely. With mixed pleasure and pain Molly saw that he was twiddling unconsciously at a piece of hair at the back of his head. Wayne always twiddled with his curls when he was shy or needed comforting.

"At least you can understand me," she murmured. "But you don't talk, do you?" He put his hand up to his mouth in a strange, forlorn little gesture.

"Oh, you *can't* talk, you mean. Well, I bet you will be able to one day," she said quickly. "We'll go downstairs now, and you can meet Maureen." He looked puzzled. "My mother," she clarified. His face brightened. "And you can meet the kittens." He put his small hand firmly in hers.

"I can't understand why you don't seem nervous with us, you know," she said. "This must be quite a shock after whatever it is you're used to. But of course I don't know what you're used to. Maybe this is a pleasant change."

Looks as if I've missed school for today, she thought. So for today at least I can keep an eye on you.

"I was just going to wake you," said Maureen, coming out of the kitchen, as Molly and Floris, hand in hand, reached the foot of the stairs. "Well," she said, beaming at Floris, "you're with us after all, are you?"

"This is my mother," said Molly. "She runs the place."

"Ha ha," said Maureen. "And ho ho. Come and

have breakfast. I thought I'd let you sleep in, Moll. You looked dead to the world when I looked in earlier."

"I couldn't help worrying about him in the night," said Molly. "But he's as bright as a cricket this morning. And you were wrong about the bruises, you know. I can't find any. He must have phenomenal healing powers." Startled, Maureen dropped onto her heels, squatting, to examine the little boy closely. As before, he waited patiently until she had finished.

"You're right," said Maureen, puzzled. "But I can't believe it. He was covered all over in technicolor bruises. As if someone had been playing football with him. Remember Wayne when he came? Well, this little one was worse. And Wayne took weeks to heal. This is beyond me, love. Upsy-daisy, Floris Gurney. Let's get some breakfast into you."

Still apparently calm and unsurprised, the little boy allowed himself to be carried into the kitchen. Perhaps he thinks he's still dreaming, thought Molly. Or perhaps they've tranquilized him so nothing worries him.

Aloud, she said: "Did I hear you say *Floris Gurney*? That sounds like instant adoption. Are you letting him stay then?"

"Well, if he's going to stay with us," said Maureen

defiantly, dispensing rounds of toast like a juggler, "we've got to call him something. And only animals and pop singers have just one name. Madonna. Fido. *People* usually have at least two. Will you just look at him, Moll? He's climbed up at the table as if he's been here all his life."

Surprisingly, Floris didn't seem hungry. He shook his head firmly at the bowl of Weetabix and only nibbled round the edges of the fingers of toast and honey Molly handed him. Then one of the kittens strolled into the room and for the first time they heard him utter a sound: a little high-pitched whoop of excitement as he wriggled down from his chair and went in pursuit.

"Careful, she might scratch you," warned Maureen automatically. But once Floris was close to Licorice, he stood stock-still and held out his hand for the skinny little creature to sniff. The kitten waited, curious to see what the little boy was going to do. Floris squatted down on his haunches and blinked several times directly into the kitten's face, in a very exaggerated, almost stagy manner. The kitten, hypnotized by now, blinked back before it could help itself. Then Floris yawned. Like the blinking it was mannered and stagy, stretching his small pointed face grotesquely from ear to ear. As though in response, Licorice yawned too, her vibrating whiskers comically outsize on her tiny black muzzle, like stiff wires. Then Floris turned away deliberately. And the kitten did the same and began washing with elaborate unconcern.

"Did you see what he did?" said Molly. "They were talking."

"Well, he's certainly watched a lot of cats," said Maureen, doubtingly. "Now, Moll, what had I better do about young Floris Gurney here? I think I should phone Social Services and see if I can get Mrs. Sutcliffe and find out if anyone knows what's going on."

"But supposing they don't let us keep him?" cried Molly in distress. Floris, his own face crumpling suddenly, ran up to peer into her face, making a pleading sea gull's mew that echoed her own frightened tone.

"He understood that," said Maureen. "You're going to have to be careful what you say in front of him. I don't think you need to worry, Moll. If he turns out not to have a home of his own, I'm sure Social Services will be happy to leave him with us. But if we don't clear up the situation legally, we may end up in trouble. In the short term, have a look in that carrier bag over there. I brought some beautiful little clothes back from that rummage sale on Saturday for Joan Naughton's little boy, but I think they'll just fit Floris. We don't want people staring at him in the street. Just in case anyone unfriendly is looking for him, it's better if we don't draw attention to him, isn't it?"

Molly tipped the bag onto the table and Floris came up curiously to look at the little pile of T-shirts, jeans, and crew-necked sweaters.

"An American football sweatshirt," said Molly swooping on the bright colors. "Not his usual style, is it? Look, these are for you, Floris." The little boy plunged a hand into the pile and came up with a bright-red cotton baseball cap, which he immediately jammed on over his eyes. "I think he likes them," said Molly, laughing. "Come on then. I'll help you transform yourself."

"Well, when he's washed and dressed, do you think you could take him into town to buy him some bits and pieces? He'll need a little pair of sneakers, and the poor mite's got no underclothes. Meanwhile I'll get things straight with Mrs. Sutcliffe."

This meant Maureen had assumed Floris was going to stay with them, thought Molly. Somehow the little boy with the dreamy violet eyes had touched her mother very deeply. If necessary she would fight for him. This was just as well, since he was going to need all the champions he could get.

CHAPTER EIGHT

A Little Flute Music

If Floris found anything unusual about taking a bus into the center of Bradley, he gave no sign of it. He sat serenely beside Molly in his rummage-sale jeans and striped sweater, the red cap tilted over his eyes, as if this was a perfectly familiar and unremarkable event. One or two of the other passengers smiled at him as they went past, and one chucked him under the chin and said what a bonny little lass she was. Molly realized that the jeweled earring and Floris's pale honeysuckle curls gave misleading signals to the straightforward folk of Bradley. But boy or girl, his delicate beauty was eye-catching whatever he wore. She reached out to the heavy jewel, fastened into his small earlobe, but before she had actually touched it, Floris jumped back from her, wincing as if she had hurt him.

"Sorry, is it sore?" she said, grieved to have upset him. "It looked so pretty that I couldn't help wanting to touch it. I'll bathe it for you when we get home if you like."

But he went on looking at her with eyes that seemed suddenly clouded with pain. There was real fear in them, she realized. Why hadn't she seen it before? He had seemed so sunny, so accepting. *It was me touching the earring that upset him.*

"Look, we're nearly there now," she said firmly, taking his hand. "I'm sorry if I frightened you. You must tell me if I do anything you don't like and I'll try not to do it. You're a clever boy. You can make me understand." He nodded and managed a smile for her and slowly the heavy hurt in his eyes retreated. "We'll get you some sneakers and some really wild underpants with Superman on them or something, and then we'll go into Mrs. Pasquale's and I'll buy you the best ice cream *Bradley Echo* money can buy. What do you say?" He jiggled her hand up and down, beaming. "Oh Floris," she said, sighing, "you're a real charmer. I hope we keep you for a good long while."

The sun shone out as they got off the bus by the old Jubilee Gardens, and Molly felt as though she was having an unexpected holiday. She knew she should be worried about Floris; that there was a chance the authorities would take him into care and that if the things the three strange visitors said were true, he might be in terrible danger and she had almost no idea what kind of danger that might be. She couldn't imagine what kind of life Floris had been living before Maureen found him. She had no idea what, if anything, he knew of her otherworldly visitors and their plans for him. But although these things occupied part of her mind, the overwhelming feeling that flooded through her was a bubbling irrational joy. She was happy today and she knew it, and nothing was going to spoil this precious morning for the two of them.

"I'm going to live for the present, like they tell you you should," she said to herself. "When I get the chance, at home, I'll try to find out what he knows. But for just this one morning, I won't think about any of it."

The sneakers Floris liked best were scarlet to match his cap, with emerald, yellow and kingfisher flashes on them. He kept them on. The saleslady put his small boots in a carrier bag for them to take home and gave Molly an odd look.

To find underwear, Molly had to brave the large, modern shopping mall, which she had always hated because it had no windows and a complete absence of natural light and air. The architects, intoxicated by Italian holidays, had obviously seen their design as some kind of piazza with splashing fountains, benches and tubs of trailing greenery. They had forgotten, thought Molly, that without the sunlight and summer air and birdsong, their piazza would remain a dull, dead imitation in which the good people of Bradley strode tight-faced, consulting their lists for cough syrup and pan scrubbers, towing their little winter-faced children unheedingly along by the arm, while the bored and wicked youth of Bradley stubbed out their cigarette ends in the plant pots and hurled their squashed beer cans in the basins of the fountains. Even so, Floris walked beside her peacefully, seeming untroubled by the crowds of people pushing past, his enormous clear eyes taking everything in.

"First the pants and then the ice cream," said Molly. "You're costing us a fortune, you know. I might have to do two paper rounds to support you." He laughed happily back into her face. He seemed to know she was teasing him.

They found the pants, but to her annoyance there was now a long line at the cash register. All at once Floris seemed uncharacteristically restless, craning his neck and frowning as if trying to hear something. Molly realized he could hear the piped music relayed over the sound system in the mall outside the store.

"It's not real music," she told him. "Just a kind of brainwashing sound they switch on to make everyone drift about in a daze and spend more money." He didn't smile this time but kept craning his neck to and fro like a trapped bird. "We'll be finished soon," she said. "I promise."

At last her turn came to pay, and she turned with relief to tell Floris they could go and get the ice cream now. But he had gone.

Molly had never felt so sick in her life. She began to run backward and forward between the cash desk and the doors of the department store scanning the shoppers frantically.

"Excuse me," she said to everyone, "have you seen a little boy with long fair hair and an earring? Oh, and a red baseball cap." And so on. Everyone was sympathetic. But no one had seen him. She flew out into the mall, cold with fear, looking around her wildly. There were hundreds of people milling around but absolutely no sign of Floris. Oh please,

please, please let me find him, she prayed. How can I have lost him so soon?

She gazed around helplessly, stunned with the shock of it. She didn't know where to start searching. Suddenly an elderly man came up to her and touched her sleeve so that she jumped and gasped, by now seeing sinister enemies in every ordinary Bradley citizen.

"Were you the lass looking for a little feller with yellow hair and an earring?" he asked kindly.

"Yes, oh yes. Where is he?"

"Well, if you go down the escalator, love, you can't miss him. I shouldn't be surprised if he's a real little Nureyev when he grows up. He's dancing down there as happy as you like."

"Oh," she said, appalled. "Thank you." And set off at a frantic run. From half way down the moving staircase she could see him, as could a hundred or so other people. In fact quite an admiring space had been cleared around him. The mall's sound system was relaying an insipid version of Greensleeves, all lush strings and angelic choirs. If Maureen had been there she would have said it took the enamel off her teeth. But gravely and gracefully, as though in some imaginary medieval ballroom, Floris dipped and swayed, courted and bowed to imaginary partners, wove and circled with them in stately elaborate measures just as though the bland and sickly strings really were playing hidden, haunting music whose power he could not resist. His cap had fallen off, and Molly just had time to notice several coins already lying inside it as she swooped furiously upon him and caught him up into her arms before he could get away again.

"Trying to do me out of business," joked a voice in her ear, and someone picked up Floris's cap for him and the paper bag containing the underwear that Molly had dropped in her dash. "This is usually my pitch, you know." Molly looked up nervously at the speaker but he was grinning back at her, a friendly face. "Let me know if he ever decides to turn pro. What a kid."

He threw his own cap casually upon the ground and took a battered penny whistle out of his pocket. "Any requests?" he asked. "No extra charge." He had jet-black hair, untidy curls that fell over his eyes, and like Floris he wore one earring: a simple gold circle. He wore a beaten-up donkey jacket and fingerless gloves: one bright pink, one turquoise, both embroidered with smiling suns.

"Can you play 'Carrickfergus'?" she asked impulsively, keeping tight hold of Floris, who seemed calm enough now in her arms and was looking with interest at the young street musician.

"Oh I wish I could," he sighed. "But I'd need another whole octave on this thing. Are you Irish then?"

"Kind of," she said shyly. "Half. My father was." The street musician had a wonderful face, like someone in a painting, she thought; it seemed always to be about to break into an extraordinarily beautiful, if unreliable, kind of smile. She had this silly feeling she knew him from somewhere. She knew she didn't and couldn't understand herself at all.

"I dedicate this to your Irish ancestry then," he said. And raising the silver penny whistle he began to play a wry sweet folk tune, pure as birdsong. Behind the piercing clarity of the Celtic air, the piped music faded down into vague, meaningless background jangle, all but inaudible. In her arms, Floris swayed his head and arms like a small windblown tree, his eyes closed, blissful until the melody ended on a wistful, questioning note. Then he opened his eyes and gazed at the musician with a strange almost yearning expression.

"Did you like that?" the street musician asked him. "I wish my audiences were always so attentive."

"He can't talk," said Molly quickly. "But he does love music. That's how I lost him. He came down here to dance to the horrible Muzak. We'd better go now. Thank you for the tune. It was lovely."

Then she looked down and found she was clutching Floris's red cap with the coins still in it. "I don't know what to do with these," she said awkwardly. "Shall I give them to you?" She was feeling ridiculous and her cheeks flamed scarlet.

"He can keep them," said the flute player. "Or give them to the charity of his choice." He grinned again, raised the whistle and began playing once more, this time a jaunty reel. A passerby threw small change jingling into the cap on the ground. Floris strained to get out of Molly's arms.

"Ice cream," she hissed in his ears. Waving goodbye briefly to the street musician, she moved away rapidly, almost running, realizing that Floris was going to be impossible whilst they were anywhere within the enchanted circle of sound cast by that battered penny whistle.

"It was so strange, Mum," she said later to Maureen. "You know how peaceful he always seems. Well, as soon as he hears music playing he isn't peaceful at all. I nearly died when I turned round and he was gone." She didn't mention the young street musician. She wasn't quite sure why, but she didn't feel ready to tell Maureen about him.

"You always used to run off in Woolworth's," said Maureen, biting off a bit of thread. She was turning up one of the pairs of rummage-sale jeans for Floris. "I usually found you by the Pick and Mix."

"So it was all right with Mrs. Sutcliffe?" Molly said for the umpteenth time. She wanted to be quite sure Floris was going to be with them for a long time.

Maureen scattered a handful of pins into a tin. "Yes," she said, patiently. "But they've got to make their own inquiries about him. They've never had a child answering to his description on their books and they've no idea at the moment who he might be. But they're going to do everything as discreetly as possible in case there's any chance that someone might want to..." She raised her head and glanced across to where Floris was sitting blinking gently at Licorice and Lucifer in turn, and didn't finish her sentence. "Do you think we should trim his hair?" she said, a vague, maternal look in her eyes.

"No," said Molly firmly. "I like it like that. He looks like a flower child."

"I just thought—about him getting noticed."

"Just a very slight trim, then," conceded Molly. "Just take the ends off the really tendrilly bits. But don't let him think you're going to touch his earring. He goes all frightened and funny about it."

"Meanwhile," said Maureen, "as you're not at school, you can get on with your homework."

"What homework?"

"Whatever homework you've got."

"What do I do if I haven't got any?"

"If you know what's good for you, you'll find you have got some."

Molly knew what was good for her. Otherwise, she reflected glumly, tipping the books out of her school bag on to her bed, she would be delegated to empty Henry Preece's wastepaper bin, or water his mold, or peel the potatoes for the evening meal. Though all these jobs were probably waiting for her anyway.

"Why is it always me," she muttered only half seriously. Sean and Cliff had never done a hand's turn at home and Maureen never seemed to expect them to. It occurred to Molly, as she settled down for another life-and-death struggle with matrices, that Maureen viewed Molly as an extension of her own person, whereas she saw Cliff and Sean as separate, detached, inexplicable creatures. Which was maybe why Maureen Gurney's voice sounded in Molly's head almost as often as it did in her own. "But I'm me," Molly thought suddenly and startlingly. And then she remembered the young street musician with the dark curls falling over his eyes and the unreliable smile and smiled herself: a private, secretive smile.

CHAPTER NINE

Floris Joins
the Real World

Over a month passed. Social Services had so far drawn a blank with their inquiries. But everyone seemed to think that the little boy had been abandoned by drifters or hippies who had somehow gotten to hear about Maureen's soft heart and ever-open door.

"After all," said Mrs. Sutcliffe gently, shifting one of the kittens off her lap as her allergy began to make her eyes itch and her nose run, "you have become quite an institution around Bradley."

"I hope not," said Maureen hotly, for whom "institution" was a dirty word.

It seemed to the professionals that Floris had

been abandoned because of his handicap. The strange note and his clothes were dismissed as pieces of inexplicable nonsense, red herrings. The social workers thought he might begin to talk once he felt properly secure. Probably he had led a confusing, distressing existence, neglected and abused by people who were themselves inadequate or disturbed. Perhaps he had chosen silence as some kind of inner protest or protection.

The flaw in this reasoning, Molly thought, was that Floris had seemed utterly secure with the Gurneys from the instant he woke up in Wayne's small white bed. In no time at all she and Floris had established together all kinds of routines—jokes, games, treats and rituals. And he understood so well what went on in her mind—her moods, her humor, her spells of silence—that it was uncanny. Each morning she woke to feel his small thin arms around her neck or an insistent tugging at handfuls of her thick frizzy hair, until she finally opened her eyes, groaning, to find his huge shining wild-violet eyes laughing into hers.

Maureen said she had never known a small child to be so little trouble. He seemed content with the simplest things: dancing to music on the radio, playing with the kittens, cutting shapes out of leftover pastry, following Maureen or Molly out into the garden to help cut the grass or hang out the washing. Even Cliff didn't object when Floris stood silently watching as he took a friend's motorbike apart and tinkered with it for hours. When Molly brought him a tub of bubble liquid with a wand designed for blowing especially enormous bubbles, he seemed ecstatic, gazing so intensely at each wobbling rainbow globe as it formed that his small white pointed face was all eyes.

He still ate little, preferring bread and honey, fruit, cheese and the apple juice Maureen bought from the health-food shop for her lodger, to anything else the Gurneys could offer. But he didn't get any thinner, so they supposed that he wasn't undernourished. Maureen remarked that he must get his food from sunlight like plants, and with a downward lurch of the heart, Molly realized how little she knew about the small boy and the world he came from. Could there be a world in which the people drew what they needed for physical existence from the energy of stars?

At first Molly had tried to question Floris very gently about his real home. When they were alone she talked to him about her three strange visitors, describing them and watching him closely for his reactions. But she got nowhere. Even when she drew pictures of them for him. She showed Floris his own strangely old-fashioned clothes, now washed and folded neatly in a drawer. He didn't respond. Her questioning just seemed to puzzle him deeply. It was as if he couldn't remember anything about himself until the moment he woke up in Wayne's old bed, in Molly's room. He watched politely as Molly talked and gestured and crayoned pictures for him, but with a strained, listening expression that made her heart ache. It was as if he wanted to please her but didn't know how. She saw in his eyes the reawakening of the heavy hurt she had seen when she reached out to touch the jewel in his ear. She couldn't bear it.

What did it matter, she thought, hugging him fiercely, protectively, when they understood each other so well in every other way and had such good precious times together? What did it matter where he came from, who he had been with? Now was what mattered. Smiling, teasing, using every means she knew to dissolve that terrible bewilderment in his wide, beautiful eyes, she began to show him how to make a paper airplane out of one of her drawings. He was Floris Gurney, her silent, magical little brother who shared more of himself with his eloquent eyes and hands than most people ever did with their clever words. What more did she need to know? She began to forget, herself, her own version of his arrival in her family, since no one but herself had experienced it. She stopped looking for her personal message from the universe in the *Bradley Free Echo*. She was no longer lonely. She was happy.

Maureen took Floris to the family doctor for a checkup, more because Mrs. Sutcliffe said she should than because she herself had any faith in Doctor Foreman. Maureen didn't believe in doctors. She believed in aspirin, peppermint tea and a good night's sleep. She didn't believe in Doctor Foreman, in particular, because he disguised his inward disapproval of Maureen and her erratic ways with compliments to her good nature, and because he had insisted Sean only had childish indigestion when in fact he turned out to have an inflamed appendix. However, Doctor Foreman agreed mildly with Maureen that unhappiness or shock of some kind might have caused the little boy to retreat into silence. He did some simple tests of Floris's hearing and intelligence and assured her that nothing was wrong physically.

"No doubt when he's ready, Mrs. Gurney, he'll start chattering away to you. He certainly seems remarkably at home with you, doesn't he?" Floris was sitting on Maureen's bony blue-denim knees, peaceably eating iced gems, which he had recently discovered and loved.

"Is he eating well?" asked the doctor as Maureen reached the door.

"As far as we can tell, he lives on iced gems and sunlight," she said enigmatically. The doctor laughed too heartily at her joke. Maureen was suddenly painfully aware of another memory that lay between her and smiling Doctor Foreman. It was when she had been heavily pregnant with Molly and had had to pretend that her bruised face and black eye were the result of bumping into a door. She had seen at once that he did not believe her but she had also seen his embarrassed eagerness to pretend he did. She left his office swiftly before the doctor could tell her again that she was a wonderful woman. Also, Floris was whimpering a little and rubbing his eye. She thought he didn't much like the doctor either.

One afternoon, Molly came back from school to find her mother looking thoughtful. She was sitting at the kitchen table, her Open University books spread out, blue smoke curling from her cigarette in evil-smelling spirals. There were toys strewn around. Shushi had been to play for the afternoon.

"Floris was squealing and laughing back at her, Moll. You know what a live wire she is. And I suddenly realized, we haven't been fair to him. It's time we sent him to playgroup."

"He's never seemed lonely," said Molly, her throat

aching suddenly with distress. "He's always seemed perfectly happy."

Some warning chord was twanging within her. She violently disliked Maureen's idea. She tried to supply reasons to herself to justify the intensity of her dismay. They were supposed to be keeping him safe, weren't they? Had Maureen forgotten that? (She had come close to forgetting it herself.) Surely introducing him to a lot of strange people might be dangerous. But maybe it was just that she preferred to think of him, jealously, as her own rare, magical little being, like a unicorn, living only with her in a shared magical world. Was that why she loathed the idea of him dashing about in toy cars and on trikes, singing, "The Wheels on the Bus" and "Five Fat Sausages" with actions. Maybe she just couldn't stand the idea of him being an ordinary rambunctious little boy.

She looked helplessly at her mother. Maureen's voice was already sounding in her head with its usual commonsensical authority.

"You think that if we let him dash about in sandpits, doing creative water play with a herd of other little kids, he might start to talk?"

"Well, he might. And he's got to learn to live in the real world sometime, Moll." Maureen Gurney had so frequently told Molly herself that she must learn to live in the real world that, hearing it once more, Molly felt herself judged and criticized all over again, through Floris's person as it were. And she couldn't bear it.

"You mean, start making guns out of Lego and zapping people and turning into a space alien like Cliff and Sean," said Molly in anguish, shamefully close to tears. "That real world, you mean?" *The world is a poisoned wasteland. The Urgs are locked in a deadly feud with the Morgs.*

"For heaven's sake, Moll," snapped Maureen, now clearly upset herself, but not giving an inch. "We're talking about St. John the Baptist Playgroup."

And so Floris was to go to the local playgroup, and on his first morning, Molly set off for school with a heavy heart: in her bones there was a low, troubled lament.

Then, as the bus swung away from the town center in the direction of her school, she glanced down, suddenly and disturbingly aware of someone staring at her. Behind her some girls giggled and nudged her. "Dark horse, Molly Gurney," said Tina Baines. "Now we know your type."

"Don't think much of his car though," added her friend.

Molly's face burned. Chugging alongside the bus was a battered green Morris Traveler, on which someone had painted in explosive rainbow lettering GREEN TIN WITCH. The driver, who was grinning up at Molly with a beautiful but entirely unreliable smile, was her flute-playing street musician whose pitch Floris had unwittingly poached. For a moment she looked away, confused. Then, impulsively, perhaps to cheer herself up as well as to impress the two giggling idiots behind her, she deliberately looked back, smiled and gave a slight airy wave. And he, as if he understood her purposes perfectly well, blew her back a kiss, managing to make it simultaneously matter-of-fact and gloriously mischievous. Then the traffic divided them and the Green Tin Witch was lost to view.

Heavens, what a face he had! And why was it that she had this crazy feeling that she knew him from somewhere? It was as if they belonged to the same family. As if they were kin to each other, yes: the same kind of people, inside. Yet she couldn't explain even to herself *what* kind of person she meant. But I do *know* him, she thought. The way I could never know Cliff or Sean in a thousand years. I could tune in to his thoughts. If I wanted to, I could even guess his name. She closed her eyes, oblivious to the odd looks from the girl sharing her seat, and let a name appear, letter by letter on the blank screen of her mind. Then she began to laugh at herself. What a total twit she was. Was she *kidding! Icarus?* Wasn't Floris bad enough?

But for the rest of the day she was serenely immune to the worst humiliations that math, chemistry or even two periods of P.E. could serve up. Perhaps she was becoming a teenager at last.

At the end of the day, she rushed home, half queasy with anxiety about Floris, but the house was empty. In the hall was her *Free Bradley Echo* bag, bulging with papers. Molly took an apple from the kitchen and set off, weighed down uncomfortably from one shoulder, her mouth full. As she reached the bottom of Vine Street, Sean and Vince pounded past her in the opposite direction, both wearing identical Nike track suits, both belonging to Vince, since Maureen could afford only Bradley factory seconds.

"Hello," she said to the empty air. Well, of course, they wouldn't answer, she said to herself. They only speak Urg; or Morg.

She did her paper round as fast as she could, all the time worrying about Floris and unicorns and what kind of world Floris might have come from and what the three visitors would have to say if they knew Maureen had sent him to playgroup so he could learn to live in the real world.

The trouble was that Molly had intense difficulty

116

thinking with any clarity about Floris. In the presence of the charismatic visitor with his dusty Hamlet costume, she had found it easy enough to believe Floris was a child from another world. That he needed her own special qualities, whatever they were, to keep him safe. Even that he was under a cruel enchantment from which she might one day free him. But once everything became ordinary again and she was drawn back into the daily routine of going to school and helping Maureen, she found herself slipping and sliding into seeing Floris as Maureen and the social workers saw him: a damaged, perhaps handicapped little boy, who needed large medicinal doses of ordinariness to make him well again: television and fishfingers, playgroup and canvas sneakers. And when he was older, Nike track suits, computer games and motorbikes.

As she trudged up paths and driveways, dodging snappy terriers, sucking her knuckles after an encounter with an especially hostile letter box, her thoughts wove back and forth uneasily. And if *they* were right about him and he does start to talk when he's learned how to be ordinary and live in the real world, she said to herself, unhappily, what will he say? Will he say, "That's my best yet?" Or make machine-gun noises? Kerboom. Zap. "You're dead, Molly."

117

She was back at the bottom of Vine Street, already unfolding her illicit spare paper, loathing the oily reek of cheap print, to sneak a look at what Tamara might have to say to her this week.

"You have made an unexpected ally: one you will surely need in days to come," said Tamara.

Molly's heart quickened. Whyever would she need an ally? Well if she did, it was just too bad, since as far as she knew she had none whatsoever. She hardly thought Henry Preece would turn out to be one in disguise, however often she watered his saucers of sprouting mold.

Swallowing, she turned to the next birthdate at the top of the next column. But something had gone wrong with the *Bradley Free Echo's* printing process. The next two columns were smudged, ink-streaked, blurred and faint to the point of total illegibility. Only one word was recognizable:

"Danger."

CHAPTER TEN

A Spellbinding Air

Molly had finished her paper round a good half hour earlier than usual, but when she got home she found Henry Preece had also come home early and was already monopolizing Maureen in the kitchen as she hastily grilled sausages for her family and simultaneously whisked up something high in dietary fiber and low in cholesterol for her stout lodger. They were discussing synchronicity, which Maureen apparently believed in profoundly and Henry Preece thought was a load of rubbish.

"It's just an excuse for sloppy, inexact, irrational thinking," he was saying.

Molly hung about tensely on the edges of this

obscure conversation for a while and then, thinking she saw a gap, plunged into it. "Was Floris all right?" she asked anxiously.

Maureen looked up exasperatedly from the eye-level grill, which for Maureen was more accurately chin-level. "Do you always have to interrupt?" she said irritably. Henry Preece peered in the mixing bowl that held his potential supper, poked in a pudgy finger, licked it and looked dubious.

"Sorry, I thought you'd stopped talking."

"But not *thinking*," said Maureen quellingly. "Well, as you're here, you can pop this pie round to Joan's husband. She's got the flu and from what she tells me, he can't boil water without using a recipe book."

"But is Floris okay?" she persisted.

"Of course he's okay," yelled Maureen, flipping burning sausages over with her bare fingers and wincing each time she scorched herself. "I told you, ouch, bloody hell, that he would be."

Tripping over the kittens who were having a friendly spat and wrestle in the doorway, Molly set off with the pie. From the living room came the sound of the television and, most unusually, Cliff's voice. "Don't want to watch this baby stuff, do yer? Let's change channels and watch the snooker. Look, I'll tell yer the rules."

Incredulously she peered round the door. Nestled up to Cliff on the shabby floral sofa, an endearing smile playing over his ethereal pale face, was Floris. Cradled lovingly in his arms was Cliff's crash helmet, and the jewel in his earring flashed tawny gold-orange. It must be the effect of the living room light. She had never noticed those colors in the jewel before.

"Look, he's going to try for a break," said Cliff suddenly. The colored snooker balls slid smoothly across the green baize. Cliff chuckled appreciatively and Floris, glancing sideways at him, chuckled too, a higher-pitched replica of the sound her brother had made. Something crept into the pit of Molly's stomach and squatted there, cold as a toad.

"Hi, Floris," she called softly. He peered round comically, his short legs swinging off the ground, and gave her a faint, gentle smile. But he didn't scramble down and throw himself lovingly into her arms as he usually did, she thought jealously. He only edged a little closer to Cliff and went back to gazing solemnly at the television screen, the jewel in his ear winking gold, orange, amber: like a tiger's eye.

"It's come!" Maureen shouted up the stairs to Molly. "The allowance for Floris has come."

Molly was not exactly up, but she was wide awake, wrapped in her huge dressing-gown, and had been for some time. She and Floris were both perched on her bed, making the puppets dance, clowning and making each other laugh.

When they finally went down for breakfast, Maureen had already got everyone's Saturday planned. She was going with Henry Preece to a country sale near Ilkley to see if she could find a sound replacement sofa for the one quietly disintegrating in the living room. Sean and Cliff would do whatever it was they normally did, and as Floris's check had come from Social Services, Molly was to take him into Bradley, get him a pair of decent pajamas and spend a bit of money on him in Hooley's, the big toy shop.

Molly was nervous about taking Floris anywhere near the shopping mall after the last time but thought she might manage the shopping without having to.

"You've come into money," she said to Floris as they rode in on the bus past the summery blossoming trees. "You're a rich man. What are you going to buy me?"

He sat serenely beside her, his hand in hers, his eyes reflecting back at her own smiling face, twinned. He was wearing a blue denim bomber jacket with TOUGH GUY embroidered in red on the pocket. Maureen had ordered it from her catalogue. He also wore a T-shirt and jeans and, incongruously, a pink-and-white bracelet of plastic popper beads he had made for himself out of an old necklace of Maureen's.

"If anyone teases you about it," she had said to him protectively, thinking of her brothers and the smaller space aliens at playgroup, "you just tell them it's your magic amulet for warding off the attentions of the Urgs. And Morgs."

At this he had touched the cheap plastic beads gravely and tenderly as if they might really have magic powers, she thought.

She enjoyed shopping with Floris. She enjoyed walking along with his small confiding hand in hers. She enjoyed the way passersby smiled at them. But she truly did not know what to buy Floris in Hooley's. A space gun with flashing lights that made a whizzing sound? A remote-control tank? She didn't think so. She couldn't think of what there was in Hooley's that Floris actually needed. He had the kittens, his tub of bubbles, now many times refueled with washing-up liquid. He had the puppets, the sandpit in the garden and all the stories in Molly's head.

They walked up and down the big store so many times that Floris began to look every bit as dazed as Molly felt. There was just too much of everything.

In the end, puritanically, she bought him a strong

mesh bag in which there were a large number of smooth, bright-colored bricks and several miniature buildings for setting up a tiny model village. There was a windmill and castle, some cottages and a farm. There were even some tiny green-painted wooden trees and some gaudy carved wooden animals. The bag was manufactured in an Eastern European country, like her own beloved theater, and was unbelievably cheap. So she still had a dishearteningly large amount of money left to spend.

"Marbles," she said, suddenly inspired, seeing some on a counter. "You'd like them, Floris. They're like little glass bubbles that don't burst. Look—they've got little twists of colored light trapped in them." As she had guessed he would be, Floris was fascinated by the marbles and carefully chose the prettiest, which the assistant wrapped for him. But the marbles were also very cheap. "Well," she said dubiously, "I don't suppose we have to spend it all today. Maybe Maureen can think of something you need."

But surprisingly Floris now tugged her across the store to a display stand studded with a great many bright badges and brooches. "What is it? What have you seen?" This kid really likes jewelry, she thought, grinning. Floris pointed excitedly to a shiny wooden badge enamelled with a brilliant fiery golden sun, like the suns in old-fashioned maps and manuscripts: the sort that have the four winds personified, puffing away round-cheeked, one in each corner. He pointed again, nodding his head and smiling hopefully. But where had she seen something exactly like that little sun badge recently?

She bought it for Floris and pinned it thoughtfully onto his jacket beside the TOUGH GUY logo. She liked the little rays dancing out round its face like fiery lion's tresses. She liked its fierce smiling face. She smiled back at it affectionately. Then she remembered. The street musician's gloves. His fingerless gloves had identical lion-haired suns embroidered onto them. At the same moment Floris was on the move again, tugging on her arm and squeaking. Near the toy drum sets, the toy pianos, the electronic organs, synthesizers and melodeons was a small storage bin crammed with penny whistles. They didn't actually cost a penny, of course, but Molly would have paid whatever it cost to see the expression on her foster brother's face as he carried his own penny whistle out of Hooley's, clutched passionately to his small thin chest.

"Do you want ice cream?" she asked Floris as they walked through the sunlit park under the fragrant snow of the cherry blossom, pigeons fluttering overhead and under their feet in a constant shudder of wings. "Or shall we go straight to get the pajamas?"

Floris strained toward the Sno Kreem van. "I agree," she said, squeezing his hand. "So all we need to know now is, with or without raspberry sauce?" He nodded furiously, beaming from ear to ear.

"Hey!" said a voice behind her. "He really does mean to put me out of business, doesn't he? He's even got his own flute now."

She looked up into a familiar, dazzling, utterly unreliable smile and her cheeks began to burn, recalling how and in what circumstances she had seen him last. But Floris was leaping with delight at the end of her arm. He wanted to show off his sun badge and his flute.

"Well," said the street musician, surprised. "You've got one of my sister's brooches. She makes all kinds. Rainbows. Clouds. Moons and stars. But she uses this smiley sun design all the time. I've even got some gloves she made me with it on. She sells her stuff on a market stall at Camden Lock in London, but I took a whole lot into Hooley's for her. Fancy you buying one."

"Is your sister an artist?" Molly asked, jealous. What a family they must be. Why did she have to land up with zombie brothers like Cliff and Sean?

"I suppose she is," he said, as if he had never really considered it. "She's always made things. I suppose it was our weird childhood. There were always people around, making little things to earn a few quid; taking a puppet show round in a box, making music." He patted the penny whistle in his pocket. "We couldn't help picking it up too."

Molly noticed that the three of them were walking together toward the Sno Kreem van. "Were you Gypsies?" she asked curiously. "Travelers?"

He laughed. "You wild romantic," he chortled. "No, I'm afraid not. My parents were sixties people: hippies, flower children. I was born when they were hot on the guru trail in India. We didn't come back to England until I was about seven. Still, I suppose that makes us kind of travelers, doesn't it?"

By now, Floris was almost bursting out of his skin to get at the ice cream van, so Molly thought she'd better turn her attention to him. But the street musician was already producing coins. "What does he want?" he asked.

"Oh," stuttered Molly, confused, "that's very nice, but I was going to have one too."

He laughed again, a warm easy sound with no mockery in it, only sympathy. "Well, I was prepared to buy you an ice cream, too, but I don't want you to feel compromised."

She hesitated. The tentative singing in her bones reminded her that she knew him to be a friend. Why should she play the silly games that other people played? "All right. I'll have a cornet, but without raspberry sauce," she said, beaming back at him.

"That's right, play it cool," he agreed. "And what about—what's your name?" he turned to the little boy.

"Oh, he can't talk," she said quickly. "His name is Floris."

"That's right. I remember now. But Florist? Sounds more like a profession than a name."

"Flor*is*," she stressed. "And he'll have the raspberry sauce."

He shuddered. "Imagine the chemicals they must use to give it that color. I bet you could see it in the dark."

"You sound like Henry Preece," said Molly. "His body is his temple."

"Quite right," he said serenely. "Mine too."

They sat on the grass by the memorial to some obscure Bradley alderman and ate their ice cream under the blossoming trees.

"Have you got a weird name as well?" inquired the musician, licking the stream of vanilla that ran down his cornet.

"Molly Gurney," she supplied. "You tell me if it's weird or not. I'm used to it, but I've been told it's clunky."

"I think it's a wonderful name," he said, staring at

her as if he genuinely meant what he said. "It goes with your Irish hair and eyes."

"And my great big feet," she agreed. He peered at her shoes, looking puzzled and then gave up. "So who uses words like 'clunky'?" he asked. "Henry Priest?"

"Preece. No. Not him. I come lower down the chain of being than lentil sprouts to him. I think it was Sophy."

"Ah, well," he said, nodding.

"You haven't told me your name," Molly said.

"That's because I always try to put it off for as long as possible," he said.

"I tried to guess it," she said impulsively. "I had this stupid idea I could guess it." Then she blushed violently.

"It's okay." He grinned, patting her hand. "You aren't compromised. You didn't have the raspberry sauce, remember? What did you guess? Though you'd better be careful, because if you get it right I stamp my foot and vanish down a hole in the ground cursing you and your descendants forever."

"I thought it was—" she shook her head, blushing again. "No, it really can't be right. I'll just have to spin the straw into gold myself like I always do." But he was still waiting, so, helping Floris to take off his tough guy jacket—the sun was really hot by the memorial—her face conveniently turned away, she mumbled, "I thought it was something like Icarus."

"Anything else?" he said, after the slightest of pauses.

Molly was almost inaudible by now. "I saw this picture of the seaside. Robin Hood Bay, it was. I told you it was crazy. You've no idea what an idiot I feel, but it's your fault for making me tell you." She was now folding and refolding the little denim jacket into neat deliberate folds.

"Icarus," he said. "Ocean. Those are my dreadful given names. But the last name you'll never guess in a million years.

At last she brought herself to look at him. He was staring at her with a stunned but delighted expression. "You mean I was *right*?"

"Oh, you aren't always psychic then? You don't make a habit of knowing things you can't possibly know about people you've only just met?"

She frowned. "I don't think so. I don't think I've ever tried before. I guessed your name! I can't believe it." Floris came to sit in her lap, leaning against her. "So what's your last name, then, that I won't ever guess?"

"If I tell you, we have to spin equal shares of the straw. And split the gold."

"Okay."

"Tomkins. That's the name."

"Icarus Ocean Tomkins," she said, marvelling. "How did you get a name like that? Did the gods name you, or something?"

Icarus lay back on the grass, a hand flung up over his eyes against the dazzling light. "My hippie parents. Or rather, my parents in their hippie phase. They wanted us to have names with *resonance* apparently, planetary resonance."

"That's the Tomkins bit, of course," suggested Molly, giggling.

"Right. Icarus and Ocean being old family names. But of course the family had to split with my dad when he called me Tomkins!"

They were laughing together like idiots. It was hard to remember they had only just met. Floris scrambled down from Molly's lap and lay down softly beside Icarus, one hand shielding his eyes from the glare in perfect imitation.

"Hello, mate," said Icarus amiably. "And how did you get such a floral name, eh?"

"We don't really know," said Molly cautiously. "He just came with it. My mum fosters him. Aren't your parents still hippies then?"

"No. All that scene fell apart in the realistic seventies, didn't it? 'The dream is over,' all that stuff.

They tried to keep it going for a while after we came back from India. We knocked around a few communes in Wales and Somerset. Then my mum got feminism. You can't blame her—"

"I wasn't going to," interrupted Molly.

"She'd been baking bread and cooking chick peas for the five thousand every day for years. And she took us off to London with her. She went back to college and got her qualifications and now she's a rich lawyer, living in Weybridge in Surrey and married to another rich lawyer. They've got two children called Georgina and Olivia." He sat up, pushing black curls out of his eyes, and began to root around in his pocket for his penny whistle.

"What about your dad?"

"What about him?" Icarus blew down the whistle harshly as if testing it.

"Has he changed too? Become a nuclear physicist or something?"

She thought Icarus seemed sad now he had talked about his family. She wondered how it felt to be such a rude reminder of someone's colorful barefoot past, when they themselves had left it so blatantly behind.

"Oh no. He's down in Suffolk in a damp cottage with a damp girl called Chloe, throwing pots that no one particularly wants to buy. I think he's all right though. He was always a bit mournful. Being a successful potter would scare the hell out of him. Come on, Floris." He ruffled the little boy's hair. "I'm going to teach you a tune on your new whistle to christen it. It's all right," he said to Molly. "Only a simple one."

Floris immediately put his flute to his lips, all attention, his eyes sparkling, dark as wood violets.

"Now, not many people know this," said Icarus seriously. "But when I was little and feeling frightened and lonely one night when we were staying in a place in Nepal—everyone was ill with hepatitis or something and there were great huge rats the size of cats and the food was pretty grim—there was a very old man staying in the same place. He was on his way to somewhere near Tibet. And he taught me this amazing thing."

Floris waited. His widening eyes seeming to take up all the space in his pale, pointed face.

"Okay," said Icarus. "Now: Everything in the universe has its own true note. Its own perfect note. Honestly. Cross my heart." For Floris had suddenly sighed, a strange and shuddering sigh, and Icarus took it for disbelief. "The stars in the sky, the crystals in the earth, the cells in our bodies, the—the baked beans on your plate! They all resonate to their own true musical tone. And when everything

133

in the world goes the way it should, all the perfect tones together make—oh—a *mighty* music, like some incredible cosmic orchestra."

"The harmony of the spheres," said Molly under her breath, repeating something that had been just a meaningless phrase before.

Icarus turned to her, delighted. "That's right. I even heard it once, you know. Not in India. As a matter of fact it was in Leicester on the most rainy miserable night you can imagine. But I heard it. It was like a vast humming top, great rippling waves of sound. But very often"—he turned to Floris—"people get sick or hurt or plain angry and mean. And then their tone goes wrong." He blew a sliding discordant wail on his penny whistle and Molly and Floris both jumped and winced. "So we musicians," said Icarus, pushing back his black hair and nodding to Floris as though to a conspirator, "have the responsibility of getting back our own true notes and helping other people find theirs. The person who told me this taught me what mine was. Listen." He closed his eyes for a moment and then hummed, a curious resonant tone, sweet and sharp at once like wild honey. The reverberation seemed to go on for some time after he had stopped humming.

My bones, thought Molly. The singing in my

bones! And as if reawakened it began again, softly, a tentative vibration of greeting.

Floris was looking pleading.

"I don't know, old mate," said Icarus. "I don't know what yours is. But until you find it, why don't you share mine? And this can be our tune. Okay?" He raised the dented and battered silver flute and began to play a simple melody in which the same three or four notes circled, returning hypnotically like a children's chanting game. Floris shut his eyes and swayed, then snapped them open and waved his own flute energetically at Icarus. "Yes, I'll show you. Put your fingers here and blow, like this."

Floris did and jumped with shock when a loud squawk escaped from his instrument. "Not bad. Do it again, but softer this time."

Molly watched, happier than she had ever been in her life, as Icarus patiently showed Floris over and over again how to play the first few notes of his tune. It sounds like a spell, she thought. It's what they mean when they say *spellbinding*. Why is this spellbinding music and the Greensleeves Muzak not? Why do words sometimes have power and other times just be useful like knives and forks, or empty like a used-up cotton reel. She was thinking of the spell she might have made herself on the night of the storm.

At last, haltingly, Floris could manage the bare bones of the melody. "And that's enough for one day," said Icarus. "You're a really clever boy, do you know that?"

"We're going to have to go," said Molly regretfully. "I've got to buy him some pajamas before we get back."

"Someone waiting for you at home, are they?"

"No. They're all out. But the potatoes are in and I've got to do them. Also vacuum."

Icarus looked at her oddly. Then he said, "We talked all about me, but not at all about you."

"That's because there's not a lot to say," she said painfully.

"You sit there with your Irish hair and your Irish eyes, Molly Gurney, having impossibly, *improbably,* guessed my name. And you say there's not much to know!" He pushed back his hair again and Floris comically did the same. "I'll come with you to buy the pajamas. I'll buy us all lunch, if you'll let me. And then I'll give you a lift home with lots of spare time for you to finish the Cinderella routine. Would that be okay?"

"Thank you," she said, shakily. "Yes, it would be nice." He stood up and held out a hand to help her to her feet.

"Green Tin Witch," she said, getting to her feet unaided. "That's what it said on your car."

"It's the name of a Heavy Metal band my sister ran around with for a while. It was her car."

"Heavy Metal van," said Molly absentmindedly. He grinned at her. His eyes were brown, she realized, but so dark they were almost black. "You have this terribly unreliable smile," she said, plaintive.

"Sorry," he said. "It's only my face. I'm actually boringly reliable, I'm told. Ask my parents. They gave me this wild spontaneous improvised upbringing and there I was, trailing around after them like a whining Woody Allen, worrying about vitamins and snakebites and how I'd ever get through school."

"So you aren't a gypsy street musician then?"

"Well, for a few months I am. Then I'm going to music college—not playing the penny whistle, idiot. I play the violin."

They were heading for a large chain store. Molly said, "But whyever did you come to Bradley? It's the back of beyond. It's *behind* the back of beyond."

"I'm staying with my mum's Auntie Dorothy," he said. "She had an operation a few months back and there wasn't anyone else to keep an eye on her. Well, no one else who could put up with her." He laughed. "Oh, *you'd* like her. She's a nutter like you. She reads the cards and tea leaves and finds lost things with a pendulum and writes the Stars column for the *Bradley Echo* or something. What's up?"

Molly had frozen in her tracks. "Does she call herself Tamara?" she croaked.

"Something like that. It wasn't her idea. It was the editor's. He thought Dorothy sounded too, er, clunky."

"How does she work them out?" asked Molly hoarsely. "The stars, I mean."

"Oh I haven't a clue. Supposedly she has charts and things. But I think she probably makes them all up, don't you?"

Molly nodded, numb. Then to her own surprise she heard herself saying as they plowed into the crowds in the store, "Have you ever heard of a word—'synchronicity'?"

"It's one of my favorite ideas," said Icarus, excitedly. And Floris bounced excitedly beside him in sympathy. "It means—oh, it's hard to explain. Like when you learn a new word and suddenly you keep seeing it everywhere. Or—suppose you painted a picture of an imaginary dragonfly and suddenly a real dragonfly flew past, and then you went home for tea and someone gave you your tea in a new mug with a dragonfly design on it, and you put on the radio just in time to hear—"

"A documentary about dragonflies," supplied Molly. "All right. I get the idea."

"I was going to say, a *song* about dragonflies," said Icarus, beetling his brows at her in mock annoyance. "Anyway the point is, when synchronicities keep happening to you it's supposed to mean you're on the right path, the true path of your life. You're slipping into harmony with the universe."

"Like Floris wanting that sun badge your sister made," she said. And your mad auntie writing the Stars column that's been sending me true messages week after week, she thought, silently.

"That's right," said Icarus. "And me playing Irish music and you having Irish hair. Molly, this is a hell hole in here. Is it going to take long?"

"Not if I can help it," she said grimly.

It didn't. She bought turquoise Dangermouse pajamas of the kind Maureen would think a little boy should have and then they went for lunch in a surprisingly nice little café that was hidden away up a shadowy side street and Icarus ordered them a beautiful vegetarian meal because he had learned to be vegetarian in his hippie days and had never managed to bring himself to eat meat since. And Floris swung his legs and sipped apple juice and nibbled a little at everything and not much at anything, and gazed solemnly and peacefully first at

139

Molly and then at Icarus with his soft wild-violet eyes, and Molly didn't think she could bear the day to get any nicer than this.

It was late afternoon when Icarus drove her to the top of Vine Street and clamped the Green Tin Witch's hand brake on hard.

"Okay," he said softly. "Well, what a nice day."

"I liked it," she agreed. "Thank you," she added, feeling herself grow hot and confused again.

And as he had done in the park he patted her hand with a sympathetic laugh. "It's all right, Molly Gurney. You never had the raspberry sauce, don't forget."

"And a very good thing too," she said primly.

"Look," he said. "I've got to go down to my dad's for a couple of days, but perhaps I could see you when I get back." He took a scrap of paper out of the glove compartment and scribbled something on it. "That's my aunt's number. If you need to get in touch with me. Or anything."

She stared at him. For a minute she had the feeling she had had with the third visitor, when she had suddenly felt as if she understood all that was happening with some deeper, wiser, *older* region of herself. She understood Icarus was offering to help her if ever she needed him to. She also knew he didn't realize himself why he had done it.

"Having another psychic moment?" he teased.

"Did you ever hear that there are some people who can travel between the worlds?" she said, hardly audibly.

"That has always seemed to me," he said, leaning across to open the door for her, "a totally reasonable concept. My sister says that what most people think is the real world is just the equivalent of one small room of all there is—and beyond that, other rooms, gardens, houses, landscapes—worlds we haven't begun to imagine. Until we begin to imagine them, we're stuck in the small room. But when we start to realize we belong to *all* the worlds, Molly—" He broke off and simply, silently looked at her with intense and disconcerting seriousness. Then he ruffled her hair lightly, almost as if she were Floris, and flashed her his original unreliable smile. "See you in a few days then, Molly Gurney."

She stood and watched as the Green Tin Witch bumped its way up the rest of the cobbles, did a lumbering three-point turn and descended again with a mighty thundering vibration, then disappeared round the corner.

Feeling inexplicably sad and alone, she looked down to find Floris clutching at a fold of her jeans, his lip trembling, his eyes filling with tears.

"Oh you silly sausage. What's the matter?" She

crouched down, pulling him into her arms, burying her face in his soft curls. But he shook his head, inconsolable. "Come on, you can set out your little wooden town on the floor while I peel the potatoes," she said invitingly. But he whimpered, clutching his penny whistle to his ribby little chest, and wouldn't put it down for the rest of the day, not even at bedtime.

CHAPTER ELEVEN

In the Castle of the Forests

Molly is getting to know the four youngest ones best, though it seems there are seven in all. There is some mystery about the seventh. Even the children won't speak of him. Everyone goes about their lives pretending nothing has happened, but tension and mystery hang in the corridors of the great castle like smoke after battle.

At first she only glimpsed the children dimly moving, like ghosts or shadows. Even when she had them in sharper focus they still looked like little figures on an old black-and-white television set. But now she sees everything in brilliant color. The colors in Launde, now that she has learned how to see them, are brighter, subtler, more varied than anything she could have imagined.

Minna is the eldest of the four. Molly thinks her cool corn-flower eyes, her hanging waist-length mass of golden curls, perfectly match the bossy big sister voice in the castle passages. Orlando comes next. The bright one. But he has a cold, slightly cruel streak that Molly would never have guessed from his wide-open innocent eyes. Like his younger brothers, he wears a crystal earring in one ear and some kind of amulet of twisted metal around one arm. Minna wears only plain gold hoops in her small, neat ears, but on a chain round her neck is a teardrop-shaped crystal as blue as her eyes. Merlin is the dreamer, the watcher: the dark-eyed silent one. Molly has a soft spot for him. Eddie is the sturdy five-year-old, with flaming cheeks, quick to temper and to tears. Desperate to keep up with his sister and brothers, always querulously demanding treats and bribes for good behavior, he is always toting about some battered eyeless rag animal for comfort. A big baby, Molly thinks. But perhaps things are different in Launde. Or maybe it's because the grown-ups in the castle, like grown-ups elsewhere, seem so much absorbed in their own secret unhappiness and Eddie is just managing the best way he can.

Molly feels as much at home in the Castle of the Forests at Launde as she does in her own dreams.

On each arrival there she feels a pleased shock of recognition, and once there she remembers at once that she has been coming here more and more frequently, and before that, for even longer, has been listening to their voices. As far as she can tell, she comes invisibly. The people in the castle go about their lives without seeming to notice or object to her. At first she has little control over which parts of the castle she visits—as though she must watch only what is shown her by some invisible film projectionist. But after a while she masters the trick of it and wanders around pretty much as she chooses.

For all its air of secrets and sadness, Molly loves the castle. It is exactly like the setting she used to imagine for Sleeping Beauty. And it is so enormous, its corridors and stairways so rambling and unpredictable, she feels she could never see all that there is to see. But Molly spends most of her time in the children's shabby apartments, though she follows them on their frequent raids on the kitchen and their boisterous shrieking games of hide-and-seek and catch that take them rushing wildly out into the neglected grounds as though blown by sudden storm winds.

One morning the castle seems unusually subdued. At first the only visible child is Eddie, who is helping his nurse make the great feather beds, solemnly and carefully, not by bouncing on them and bundling himself giggling in the bed curtains as he usually does. Then Molly hears the sour nasal tones of the tutor in the schoolroom, teaching the children the geography of Launde.

"Correct, Merlin. I'm relieved someone has woken up at last. The name 'Launde' actually means 'the place between two forests'. It is usually referred to as the Kingdom of Launde, but as you will know, the Royal Household has nowadays largely ceremonial duties only. The true power in the kingdom for several hundred years now has been divided among—whom, Minna?"

"The Seven Families, sir."

Molly peers round the door and grins to see Minna with her golden hair wound round her small neat head in tight gleaming braids, her face shining and good.

"The Seven Families. That is correct. Of which my Lord Gilbert and my Lady Agnes's household at the Castle of the Forests is one, of course." At this point the crabbed little tutor gives a faint, mock-deferential bow and Molly sees Orlando's face contract into a fleeting scowl, swiftly camouflaged with a wide, innocent smile.

"And my Lord the Magus and Lady Eleanor of Harper's Ford is another, of course," Orlando contributes, in a perfect impersonation of the tutor's own inflection, his gray eyes wide and innocent as his smile.

The tutor's expression changes rapidly. He opens his mouth as if to protest or reprimand Orlando for some appalling impertinence, but at this point Molly hears a faint choking sob somewhere behind her and is distracted. She wanders back along the corridor barely registering the angry argument that has broken out between Orlando and his tutor in the schoolroom.

She finds a small passage leading off the central corridor and notices a door left ajar. Again she hears a muffled sob and this time a slight movement. Molly slips into the room. It is a child's nursery but stripped of a child's playthings and clutter. Seated on a low stool, by the hearth in which no fire is lit, is Lady Agnes, her head bent, her arms cradling some tiny white baby clothes. She rocks to and fro as though she still holds a living child, her face drained white as bone, her eyes burning, dry and tearless. Molly goes out quickly, feeling for the first time guilty of spying. Confused and unhappy, she wanders aimlessly up and down passages and stairways until she finds herself in yet another unfamiliar part of the castle.

She walks on and on, uncertainly, yet as though drawn by a spell. Through an archway, up three little worn steps and through a doorway which seems much older than the rest of the castle. She feels so strange, so dreamlike is her progress, so secretive the atmosphere, she can almost imagine that she will open a door onto a room in which an old crone is spinning with an enchanted spindle. But instead she finds herself in a large sunlit book-lined study. By mistake she has wandered into my Lord Gilbert's chambers.

My Lord is standing by a narrow window, looking out into the glorious morning without appearing to see it. He is not a particularly tall man, though he is broadly built and muscular. If he were not one of the Seven Lords of Launde, she might have imagined him to be a blacksmith or a soldier. His hair is bright red-gold, flaming in the sunlight, and his anger, too, burns around him in a steady furious flame.

Bad enough that this curse should fall on his household in his lifetime, but that his wife should dishonor them all and seek to escape the consequences—Molly hears his thoughts as clearly as if spoken. So this is the husband of Lady Agnes, the one who blames her "for all."

"It's not her fault," she says aloud. "He's only a little boy, you know. And you wouldn't help her. You wouldn't even talk to her. She loves him. She tried to do something to save him. You were too busy sulking *and blaming everyone else—and still are, to look at you."*

He swings round, glaring, and she thinks for the space of a faltering heartbeat that he knows she is there. But he doesn't seem to see her. In some strange way, though, he responds to her words as if she has put uncomfortable thoughts into his head. He sits down heavily at his great carved desk and looks blindly at the objects littering its surface. He sinks his head into his hands. His beard is red-gold and rather disordered like his lion's-mane hair. Molly decides he might look quite human, even rather nice, if only he weren't so resentful and so dreadfully sorry for himself.

"She has put us all in danger," he says aloud. "Shamed and dishonored us all. And for what? A breathing space, it can be no more. There is no hiding place from the Lord of Harper's Ford. Nothing can be hid from his serpent's eyes. Fueled with centuries of hate, the Magus will hunt the child down with his foul arts, like a hound of hell. Better for us all—aye, even for the babe— if the midwife had strangled the child at his birth. My Lady should have yielded him up. It is the Law. Now what will become of us, what will become of the Kingdom if one of the Seven Families flouts the Law? It is enough that we have been set one against the other all these—" And he is up again, pacing at the bright window.

Molly is shivering violently, though she doesn't know why. From her brief moment of almost liking Lord Gilbert for his lion's hair and ruddy open face, she is now furiously contemptuous of him.

"Well, at least she has some courage!" she yells at him, flinging away all caution, shaking all over with emotion. "You might have the face of a soldier and the hair of a lion and call yourself a great lord, but inside, you're only a—You've only got the dull mind of a milk cow," she finishes up, ridiculously, remembering what Lady Agnes had said. "At least she isn't a quitter!"

He turns on her now, his face blazing wrath, his knuckles whitening as he clenches them, but already he is blurring like a bad television picture, already Molly is opening her eyes, perplexed, hearing her own voice yelling out, wondering vaguely what she has been dreaming. Her alarm clock shrills. Today it's the school trip to the Industrial Museum on the other side of Bradley.

CHAPTER TWELVE

The Eyes of
the Magus

Molly wished that she didn't have to go on the school trip. But Maureen had already paid out the nonreturnable cost of it. She had no choice. She had always hated going anywhere in great groups and gangs of schoolchildren. Hated being herded into lines and talked at and made to write everything down on stupid clipboards. The only worthwhile thing she had ever learned from school trips was how to hypnotize herself into not being sick on the coach. And, she supposed, the words to several dubious songs sung loudly and raggedly on the way home. This morning she had a headache that had attached itself like an invisible limpet somewhere over her left eye. She felt obscurely troubled. Funny how you could feel really terrible all day, just because you'd had a bad dream, even though you couldn't remember what it was you'd dreamed about.

"Why have you got to go, anyway?" said Sean, irritated with her as she gloomed about the kitchen, making herself some very unappetizing-looking sandwiches. She slid them into a greaseproof bag, hoping she'd feel more like them nearer the time.

"I told you. We're doing the Industrial Revolution."

Sean was in a good mood. He was off to a computer exhibition in London. This inclined him to be sympathetic.

"I've had at least three trips to that dreary place," Molly said, counting them off on her fingers. "One at Junior School, then Middle School and now this one. Why do we have to keep going? It's not even as if there's anything much to *see*."

"Well, there's the old millstones outside," began Sean. "And the waterwheel, and the power looms. Vince nearly got his hand stuck in one once. That livened it up. But what else is there?"

"There's the little cottage restored to look like the real thing, a real weaver's cottage," said Molly. "That's nice. With the fire burning in the grate and the old lamps and the patterned quilt on the bed."

"I still don't see how they're going to take all day to show you round it," he said. "Unless you go round in slow motion." He mimed it for her, swimming slowly across the kitchen, mouthing silently like a fish and colliding with Maureen, who looked quite shocked to have caught her son and daughter having an amicable conversation but didn't like to say so.

"Bit pale this morning, Moll," was all she said. "Didn't you sleep well?"

The school coach took them in the direction of Rustling Lane. Molly couldn't prevent herself from looking out of the window as the coach passed Albert Villas. It was there, her octagonal tower, shimmering in its own mist, fringed with forest; "...the place between two forests..."—where was that from? As the coach plunged off toward the ring road, Molly registered a For Sale sign outside one of the villas. She sank back in her seat, deep in her own thoughts.

"Michelle saw you in the park on Saturday," Sharon Petry called to her insinuatingly from across the aisle. Molly frowned, wanting to be left alone.

"Molly Gurney loves hippies," said Sharon contemptuously to the coach at large.

"You're right," said Molly wonderingly, unconscious of the giggles and rolled eyes of her classmates. And tinkers and gypsies, she thought. Wanderers, travelers—the *unbelonging*. Where had she heard that word? She knew that it didn't mean people who drifted through their lives belonging to nothing at all, like solitary human sycamore seeds whirling in space, never taking root. She thought that it might mean something like another kind of belonging, that was all, a different kind that was deeper and wider. A kind that, instead of shrinking you down to fit it, swept you up and showed you that you were really part of some mighty music that had always been there and would always be there. All at once her mind was leaping excitedly across distances like a comet. She had a brief electrifying awareness of forests, oceans falling away from her and then stars. And beyond the stars were stars, worlds, moons, suns into infinity. Dazed, she shook her head.

Michelle was leaning forward now, eyes gleaming, teeth sharp and white as a small hamster's: "She gets it from her mum," she said, amused. "My mum said she'll have any old flotsam and jetsam in her house."

Molly was vaguely taken with the phrase "flotsam and jetsam" and thought it sounded like a music-

154

hall act. Icarus would think it was funny. He's like me, too, she thought. One of the *unbelonging*. But who are we? And what are we for? She blinked hard, sternly sending away returning dizzying vistas of forests, oceans, stars. Instead she thought of her mother, Maureen, with her tough talk and her soft heart: her hatred of petty rules, petty authorities and institutions. She grinned. Maureen couldn't even open the Weetabix packet where it said "Open this side up" and would never read the instruction manual for any piece of household equipment on principle, preferring to muddle her way through precariously with a mixture of intuition, common sense, and sheer good luck.

Anxious to survive childhood, her daughter had learned how to wire an electrical plug at the age of ten. Suddenly Molly had a vision that took her breath away of Maureen as a kind of stubborn glorious hybrid of poet and amateur plumber, banging defiantly on the pipes of the universe to hear her own personal unmistakable resonance come singing back. Perhaps it was no accident that Maureen's house stood on the windy hilltop level with the wild moors, with all the busy smoky town spread out below and the overgrown orchard running wild at the back. Perhaps she was her mother's daughter after all.

The Industrial Museum was on the outskirts of Bradley, within sight of a long disused colliery and on the edge of particularly bleak moorland. Molly had always loved what she thought of as the "real moors," with their sweet heather-scented air and yellow gorse, their gleaming fat cushions of bilberry bushes, the wild lark song. But this: She shivered violently as she stumbled off the coach just behind Sharon Petty. Here nothing grew amongst the blasted-looking dun grass but frail white cottony wisps of some plant she couldn't identify. Here was the perfect setting for the witches from Macbeth. But instead there was a collection of dour cottages and old mill buildings, some newly built stairways and connecting walkways, and a raw-looking one-story building of new stone that housed the gift shop. And a wind sweeping across the desolate landscape straight from the Russian steppes.

Still impaled on her spike of headache, Molly followed her allotted group around in a reluctant daze. Whenever Miss Aimes said something in a particularly loud or emphatic voice, she wrote it down dutifully on the sheets of paper fastened to her clipboard. She felt unreal, as if the important part of her were worlds away. She thought about the octagonal tower at Albert Villas and wondered when she had first noticed it. This thought flowed confusingly into a dream or memory of a bright fire of driftwood on an open hearth and a man with silver-streaked hair and a hawkish face. The Keeper. This flowed into the image of an unhappy woman in a hooded cloak, thrusting her shaking hands angrily behind her back. And then the same woman rocking, rocking tearlessly, nursing in her arms a small white bundle of baby clothes.

Then it was as if an invisible spring, which had been winding itself tighter and tighter without her knowledge, suddenly reached its limit and she gasped and she knew, and she said aloud: "Floris!" Understanding flooded her like sunlight pouring into her mind, illuminating all the shadowy broken fragments, all the separate, warring elements of her life, showing them to be one, complex but whole. She understood who Floris really was and that his world was not a place to be traveled to through time or space, or broken into through wardrobes or pantries, whatever she had half believed. No. Somehow the magical world he came from occupied the exact same space as her own dull unremarkable life at school and home in back-of-beyond Bradley.

It was simply that she was having to learn to *see* what was there all along. She only had to learn how to shift her focus—she could almost remember now what she needed to know. She was standing stock-still outside the building that housed the looms, oblivious of the people jostling and pushing impatiently past, and the deafening sound of the looms as the huge shuttles pounded to and fro.

"Aren't you well?" asked Miss Aimes concernedly, seeing Molly apparently frozen, her face drained of color. "Perhaps you should give the looms a miss for now. There's a little café in the exhibition room. Why don't you get yourself a cup of tea and wait for us there. It'll soon be time for lunch."

Grateful to escape, Molly nodded and mumbled something appropriate and found her way numbly into the café. She bought herself a cup of surprisingly orange tea and went to sit with it by a display of old photographs of Bradley mill girls and Midlands hosiery workers, warming her icy hands around the polystyrene cup.

Her headache was blinding. Her moment of pure clear vision had gone. Why did it come and go so maddeningly? What was it she had almost understood? "...A place between two forests...."...Floris... He was...Other worlds shimmering within and interpenetrating her own. If she could just learn how to *see*.

She sat holding her poor throbbing head, her gaze roaming around the little ground-floor café.

Around the upper portion of the room ran an attractive gallery of modern pine, reached by a staircase. She could smell the newness of the varnished wood. Perhaps there were other displays up there. If only she could remember what it was she did when she *saw*. What exactly was it that happened when the octagonal tower came into focus?

Then the air darkened and shimmered and she saw him. It seemed as though he was really there, looking down on her from the gallery, but she knew he watched her from another place, another world. She knew him at once from the figure in the tapestry, howling like a beast over a girl's body. But the man in the tapestry had still been recognizably human in his grief and range: an anguished father. This Magus was no longer a man but a shriveled old monster. On his stooped, shrunken body, the rich clothes hung emptily like a gaudy coat on a scarecrow. His hair was bright as frost, but his face was drained of all human color except for a fever flush like rouge on his high prominent cheekbones. Under hooded deep-set eyes were shadows like great bruises. The Magus of Harper's Ford was a dying man, eaten by his own darkness and dread. The expression in his eyes chilled Molly.

For the space of several heartbeats she shrank

159

back from it as from a dark icy flood in which she might drown. She was his enemy and he had found her at last. Then she sprang to her feet, knocking over her cup, opening her mouth to cry out that he was mistaken. It was a terrible mistake—he was not her enemy nor she his. She wanted to implore him to understand that nothing he could do to Floris could root out the hungry pain that ate away at his own body hour by hour. But as if she was trapped in a nightmare, no sound would come. She started toward the staircase, began to run up the polished stairs. She would reach him. She would tell him why he need not harm Floris. She would explain and he would listen—but with a smile of naked contempt the Magus turned and vanished into a dark glittering of air.

Mechanically, Molly made herself return to the café, where she bought a second cup of tea. Mechanically, she later rejoined her class for the rest of the tour. After lunch she viewed, without seeing, some women dipping candles and hanging them to dry by their looped wicks. She walked sightlessly around the weaver's cottage and the adjoining property with its pig, hens and little Dexter cow. She tramped up the Nature Trail to the disused gravel pit, now an artificial lake, and tramped back again, not even shivering in the cutting wind that swept across the dull-brown moor. All she could see was the dark flood that waited to drown anyone who looked into the Magus's eyes. And now he had found her, and through her, Floris.

CHAPTER THIRTEEN

Darkness in the Mirror

Several days passed. At first Molly felt haunted by her experience at the museum. But slowly it became for her one of those inexplicable personal things which had happened only to her, could not be shared or explained and so, perhaps, was not *real* in any important sense.

Despite his promise, Icarus did not appear. Molly had the piece of paper with his aunt's number on it, but she didn't like to telephone in case, secretly, Icarus had been laughing at her all the time. She had had a wonderful, magical day with him, but like the octagonal tower, the three visitors and the magician at the museum, it could not possibly have been real in the usual way. She toughened herself against the hurt, something she had become good at.

Then one day Molly came home from school to hear the familiar but faint sound of a flute floating from her own house. Her heart leaped. It was his tune! The hypnotic, circling, spellbinding air he had begun to teach Floris in the park. Maureen had the radio on loudly in the kitchen while she made pastry and had no idea what Molly was talking about when she dashed in breathlessly demanding, "Who's that playing?"

"One of the boys?" Maureen suggested indifferently, cutting out pastry leaves and roses.

Molly took the stairs two at a time. The music grew louder. It was unmistakably Icarus playing. As she reached the top of the stairs the tune stopped abruptly in midphrase. "Icarus?" she said, ridiculously, pushing open her bedroom door. Floris, squatting on the floor with his penny whistle, looked up at her, smiling.

"Was it *you* playing?" demanded Molly, angry and incredulous and violently disappointed all at once. "But you couldn't remember it when I asked you to play it for Mum. You *couldn't* have been playing it."

He gazed at her, then shrank back. She realized how large and angry she must look and sound to him. She had never shouted at him before.

"It's okay, sunbeam," she said quickly, hugging him tight. "It's just that I was walking along with this tune in my head and suddenly I heard the tune *outside* my head as well and I thought, well I probably wanted to think... Never mind. I'm a complete fool. Let's get the marbles out and I'll show you a good game."

But she was shaken. She had been sure she had heard Icarus.

The next day the trouble began.

As soon as she opened the door she knew something was terribly wrong.

"How was Floris?" she said at once, fear and foreboding flooding her. "How was he, at playgroup?"

Maureen was angrily cleaning out cupboards on her hands and knees. "Oh *he's* fine," she said, with odd emphasis. "*Floris* is fine."

Frightened, Molly peered in the living room where Cliff and Floris sat together on the Gurneys' new secondhand sofa and he did look fine, if a little paler than usual.

"Floris?" she called, her voice catching. He swiveled to look at her and smiled faintly, the jewel in his ear a tawny tiger's eye, and then looked back at the screen. Well, there was nothing visibly wrong, was there, to alarm her so badly? Her heart beating loudly in her ears, she went back to the kitchen.

"So what's wrong?" she pleaded. Fifteen years of being plugged into the 24-hour-a-day radio station that was her mother had made her acutely sensitive to Maureen's moods.

Maureen always froze up in a crisis and had to be patiently thawed like a supermarket chicken before she'd divulge her real thoughts and feelings.

Supper was anguish. The jangling of Molly's bones told her how very wrong things were. Maureen had changed somehow. She was not unkind to Floris. She didn't even ignore him. But a glittering distance had grown up between them like a spreading frost. Molly's cutlery screeched across the plate. The inno-cent sound of her own chewing deafened her. Henry Preece held forth, she supposed about the govern-ment. She saw his mouth open and close and heard the sounds stream out of it. But her attention was all fixed on Floris, so white and bewildered, and Radio Maureen broadcasting silent storm warnings for all she was worth. By the end of the meal Molly was exploding with tension.

"Please," she said quietly when they were alone washing up, "please tell me what's wrong." Maureen went on, savagely sluicing grease and tomato sauce

165

off the chipped china plates with a raging torrent of scalding water from the tap.

"He's more than I can handle," she said at last, her lips tight.

"You mean Floris?" said Molly in disbelief. It was as if a river had reversed its flow to the sea. It was like the stars going out one by one because someone hadn't paid their electricity bill. It was—Molly felt her known world falling round her ears.

"I've never had to deal with a violent child," said Maureen. "And I don't mean to start now." She slammed plates onto the draining board one after another.

"Violent?" repeated Molly, disbelieving. "Which of us is going barmy, Mum?"

Maureen took a deep breath. She was nearly thawed now. Any minute she was going to tell Molly exactly what had happened, and Molly was growing less certain every second that she wanted to know.

"He attacked another child at playgroup," said Maureen, a tremor in her voice. "Hilda Johnson's son. The one they had so much trouble with at the start. Danny did something, apparently—I don't know, teased him or tried to touch his precious earring or something—no one seems to know

166

exactly, it all blew up so suddenly. Next minute Floris was going berserk; screaming, biting, kicking—"

"*Floris?*" Molly repeated numbly. "It isn't true, Mum. They've made a mistake."

"It took *three* helpers to drag him off," Maureen plowed on remorselessly, "*three helpers*, to drag him off and hold him down until he'd calmed down. *Three!*"

Molly was silent, feeling stunned and sick.

"I went down to fetch him, Molly. They rang me. One of them said to me when I got there, 'Well, of course you don't know anything about his background, Mrs. Gurney. Maybe the people he's been used to behave like that every time they suffer life's ordinary little setbacks. You'll have to watch him; he's a disturbed child,' she said. She said she'd always thought he was much too quiet and docile. Just biding his time, she said. Cunning and secretive, she said. She said, 'At least you know where you are with a real boy like Danny.'"

"That's true," said Molly with feeling. "He's a hideous little thug."

"Well, he's had to have three stitches in his arm down at Bradley Infirmary," said Maureen, wiping her eyes quickly and groping for her cigarettes, "where Floris bit him. But, Molly, when I went to fetch him, he came to me as sweetly as if nothing had happened. Just put his little hand in mine and smiled up at me with those great drowning violet eyes. Oh, he looked pale and ill, but not especially guilty or anything. There's something the matter with him, Moll, and I can't deal with it."

"That's just silly," said Molly before she could prevent herself. "You're tired. You don't really mean it. You've had dozens of mixed-up children before. You always coped with them. This is just silly."

"But it was always all out in the open before," said Maureen.

Molly had rarely heard such an edge of distress to her mother's voice.

"Even when they were being deceitful I could always understand why. They were just ordinary unhappy children who'd been hurt. They lied, they stole from my handbag, they wet the bed, they kicked and punched, they—they put the cat in the washing machine. But Floris—Molly, he seems so quiet. So peaceful. On the surface he seems like the most angelic child I ever met—and yet—he did this terrible thing. There's something wrong with him, Molly. Something deeply hidden and wrong. It's as if—you were sitting one moment by a peaceful pool on a summer day and suddenly—something—*dreadful* rose up out of it. Something—" She gestured helplessly, unable to make herself put it into words.

Molly began blinking rapidly. She bent down hurriedly and began to untie and retie the laces on her sneakers unnecessarily tight. Anything to shut out whatever loathsome image Maureen might inadvertently send via her infallible mother-daughter telepathy. She didn't want Maureen's image of Floris as a marred angel, but it rose up before her all the same. She violently rejected Maureen's version of Floris as a treacherous smiling summer lake in which something unspeakably abhorrent waited coiled in the mud. But how could she defuse it of its power?

Gathering courage she said, "He hates anyone touching his earring, Mum. You know he does. It was that. Bet you anything you like, it was that. Mum, trust me—I *know* it was just because of the earring. Sometimes I do know things. You know I do. Like where your wedding ring had rolled to in the bathroom. And when grandma died. Someone must have hurt him really badly once. That's what it is. Something really terrifying he can't tell us about— but he *would* if he could speak. It isn't fair, is it—" Molly's voice was rising. She was growing hot in the face. "You can make up anything you want about him and he can't contradict you because he can't speak. There isn't anything sinister about him, Mum. I just know there isn't. It's because of my dad that you're frightened Floris will turn out violent."

169

The heat had left her face. She was startled to hear her voice releasing these words. Like a small flock of unfamiliar birds, they were let loose in the room with a disturbing life of their own. Once again she had spoken with some ancient knowledge she hadn't known she possessed. She felt the dangerousness of her own hidden power.

Maureen shivered suddenly and wrapped her arms tightly around herself, staring at Molly as if she didn't know her. "Haven't you heard anything I've been saying?" she demanded in a hoarse voice utterly unlike her normal one. "I think Floris is severely disturbed. He needs special care. He's beyond anything I can do with a spank or a cuddle or a dose of peppermint tea. For heaven's sake, Moll—I can't go on and on forever looking after other people's stray puppies. It's about time I started to look after myself."

But why must poor Floris be the first person apart from me that you practice saying "No" to, cried Molly in inward anguish.

"Henry's asked me to marry him," said Maureen suddenly. It was clear she hadn't meant to tell Molly this at all, but as usual with Maureen, the flood following the thaw bore all kinds of other unexpected things bobbing along with it. She gave a weak giggle. "Well, I mustn't put words into his mouth.

His actual words were 'Perhaps we ought to regularize the relationship.'"

"You wouldn't!" Molly had actually backed physically away from her mother, her face distorting with revulsion.

"I don't suppose I would," agreed Maureen calmly. "But I have to start thinking of myself. You lot won't be around forever." She hummed a defiant little tune to herself as she wiped around the sink and draining board.

Oh, she couldn't ever pick a decent man, could she? Molly raged to herself as she stumped up the stairs on her way to put Floris to bed. She's escaped from a man who might have *beaten* her to death, now she's chosen one who'll bore her into the same condition.

She could hear the bleep of Sean's computer. Since his visit to the exhibition in London, he'd taken to trying to write his own adventure games and was planning a golden future for himself as a software millionaire. Fleetingly she let herself think of Icarus: his dazzlingly beautiful grin, his anxiety about vitamins, his silly fingerless gloves with their embroidered smiling suns. Supposing I phoned his mad auntie, she thought. I could always go and have my tea leaves read. And sort of bump into him accidentally. You're pathetic, she told herself. This is teenage behavior. Cut it out. Spin your own straw into gold from now on.

Floris's routine at bedtime was always the same. Once he was cozily tucked in, Molly would read him a story or, more often, tell him one out of the thousands roaming loose in her head. Wayne used to say to her: "Will you read me one of the stories out of your head, Moll?" And when she had finished, Floris would hug and kiss her just as Wayne used to do, and then simply turn on his side and fall asleep, apparently instantly, the way Wayne did. It was Chantal who had had the night terrors. Strange how like Wayne Floris was in some ways. Even down to a shared passion for iced gems. But Wayne had never hurt anyone so badly that they needed to have three stitches. Wayne had never hurt anyone at all, so far as Molly knew. Floris lay calmly in his narrow white bed, in his new turquoise pajamas, and waited for Molly to choose a story. It was impossible to think of him as a violent child. Molly felt herself melt with love for him. Sometimes, though she could never have admitted this, she secretly pretended he was her own little boy. In the soft glow of the bedside lamp, the jewel in his ear pulsed like a small star: rose, lavender, diamond white.

Without consciously deciding to, Molly began to

tell Floris the story of Elise, whose seven brothers were changed into wild swans by her stepmother's wicked enchantment. He lay, listening intently, his eyes fixed dreamily on her face as if, she thought, he could really see the vivid pictures passing through her own mind. It was such a sad, haunting story but she had always loved it. She loved to imagine the seven brothers transformed from princes into seven wild birds: Elise, in her hidden forest home, keeping her long silent vigil, spinning magic cloth out of nettles for shirts to set her brothers free from the spell forever. But I don't know how she could marry that stupid king, she thought, not when he was going to have her burned as a witch before.

She looked across at Floris. Drifting into her own thoughts, she had forgotten him. He had fallen asleep, his small hand drooping open outside the covers, his breathing soft and steady.

Oh, Floris, she thought, how can I rescue you? If I knitted you a little magic shirt out of nettles, would it break the spell? Would it unfasten your tongue and set you free?

She had no inclination to go downstairs and get on with her homework. Maureen had gone out for the evening with Henry Preece to an extra tutorial, her hair newly washed, her eyelids faintly hyacinth, her freshly ironed blouse giving out little shock waves of perfume, her smile so brave and bright that Molly was irresistibly reminded of visits to the dentist.

Sighing, Molly picked up her hairbrush and began brushing hard at the reddish frizzy bush of her hair. Lately she had begun to think that it might not be so hopeless after all. Irish hair, she thought, wistfully. Irish eyes. In the small mirror she could see, framed, her own ordinary sensible face and behind her, Floris's small head and shoulders turned vulnerably toward her on the white pillow.

Then several things happened at once.

The reflection of Floris's earring in the mirror seemed suddenly to expand like an opening eye, and as it grew it began to flash violently through a harsh new spectrum of colors, ending on a blazing dark blood crimson that was almost black. Simultaneously, the hidden and forgotten singing in her body burst into an anguished concerto of protest and alarm. At the heart of the mirror a glittering darkness began to gather. Within the darkness someone was looking back at her out of the mirror. That he was as yet invisible made no difference. He was calling to her. If she allowed herself to focus her thoughts on him, if she let herself imagine him as he had been that day at the museum, he would appear in her room with a glittering disturbance of air like a dangerous frost. Tearing her mind from his, and her fascinated eyes from the darkening mirror, she turned with a cry of terror toward the bed. For just a second, perhaps only a fraction of a second, the reflected Floris, sleeping in his Dangermouse pajamas, had vanished. His outline fuzzed and he simply vanished, like a light going out. But she must have imagined it. She was so frightened she was seeing things. There he still lay, the jewel in the earring shrunk back to its normal size, already winking softly down through its old gentle spectrum, rose, lavender, white.

But I know someone was looking at me through the mirror, she thought in horror. And in revulsion she tore the little mirror off its hook and turned its face against the wall. As an afterthought she also draped an old school cardigan over it.

The Magus has found a way into our world. He has found a way into our home, to find Floris and hurt him, she thought, trembling all over. She stood in the middle of the room, unable to make a move in any direction. She was breathing in great panicky gasps. *Slowly*, she said to herself. *Breathe slowly. Think. What's the best thing to do?* But it was no use. She was terrified. Why did the earring grow so big? Why did it change into that hideous color like a burning coal? Like *blood*. She realized that she felt violently cold all over; from the crown of her head to the soles of her feet she was freezing. Her fingernails were mauve. "Not your best color, dear," she told herself, her voice wavering on the edge of tears. Hardly knowing what she was doing, she undressed and crept into bed, wrapped in Maureen's old dressing gown, not caring that it was early. It's a magic earring, maybe, she comforted herself, her teeth chattering, her skin prickling. Maybe it's just protecting and guarding him against the Magus. So I needn't worry.

But still she lay in a tense, curling crouch as if she might have to spring up at any moment and fight for their lives. But as the moments passed, agonizingly slowly, then half an hour and at last an hour and still nothing happened, she allowed herself to find a more normal position for her cramping limbs. But still she watched in terror for herself and Floris.

She lay so long, watching and waiting, that after another hour or so she arrived almost, but not quite, on the edge of sleep: a blurred border country in which dreams drifted up close enough to touch.

Images created and dissolved themselves. The huge jewel like a burning coal. The mirror with its gathering darkness within which their invisible enemy watched. The youngest swan brother, for whom Elise only had time to make a shirt with one sleeve, so that forever after he had to live as a man with one human arm and one white pinioned swan's wing.... How could she rescue Floris? How could she free him? How could she show Maureen she was wrong? She was no longer Molly but Elise and he was her little swan brother. She would watch over him forever in the forest. Exhaustion took over her mind. She began to see things that could be neither real nor possible as her eyelids, flickering, fell and rose, fell again.

Floris's outstretched arm began to blur, change, dissolve like something fluid, re-creating itself in soft gleaming ivory until it seemed now to have become a small fluttering wing. She saw each feather clear, separate and sharply perfect as though by moonlight. Swan feathers.

Then she shot upright, sick with fear, suddenly understanding what she had seen, her heart pounding as though it would burst out of her chest. The dream fled. His small hand with its pink nails, carefully cut short by Molly herself only yesterday, lay curled open, trusting. His eyelids quivered and his lips moved without sound. He was dreaming. He was a small beautiful child smiling at someone in his dream. How could she have recoiled from him? He had brought her such happiness. He had had such inexplicable troubles in his short life. What would happen to him if Maureen gave up on him? How could she keep him safe? Icarus had liked Floris but Icarus had gone away. She was all Floris had. If she no longer loved him, what would become of him? This thought terrified her as if it were not her own. As if something formlessly dark and glittering had leaked out of her mirror and into her room and was now trying to find its way inside Molly. *Stop it!* she told herself angrily. Of course she loved him. She loved him still. How could she even imagine no longer loving him? She lay down again and wrapped the covers more closely round herself. She had simply been dreaming too. But it was several lonely hours before she slept again.

CHAPTER FOURTEEN

A Splinter of Ice in the Heart

Someone is telling her some kind of story, but she feels too ill to listen. She has to do something. She has to remember something. She mustn't let...But the voice is so insistent. Listen, it keeps saying, almost singing. You have to understand. She tries. She really does, but she feels so terrible. Icy cold and bruised all over. As if she has been in a street fight. She is aching, sick. She can't follow the voice at all. Who is this bullying and lecturing her when she wants so badly just to let go and sleep? But she mustn't sleep. That's dangerous. If she lets go... the Magus could—The voice has almost finished the story—or was it a riddle? Why does she feel so terribly sad? Why does she just want to cry and cry? "Do you understand what was broken?" But she hasn't heard all the story and she doesn't know the answer to the riddle and she doesn't understand anything. She has never understood anything. . . .

Molly woke suddenly with violent cramping in her gut. It was still early: only a faint light stole through the curtains. It was the pain that had woken her, pain shrieking in every limb and convulsing in her stomach. And worse. She lay weakly, washed over by the most appalling nausea she had ever had in her life. It was as if she had been struggling all night with something or someone unseen. Oh no, she pleaded silently. Just let me get to the bathroom first.

She did, just. Afterward she crouched weakly on the bathroom floor, her burning cheek pressed against the porcelain tower of the old-fashioned washbasin, knowing that for some time it was futile to go back to bed. Over and over she was sick. She began to be afraid she would die. As it went on, she wished she would. Her skin burned with fever but she was so very cold. *A splinter of ice in my heart.* Why did that keep running through her head? What was that story? Again she was sick. Again she felt a strange, distant relief as if she was cleansing herself of something deadly.

She heard a footfall and managed to turn her head. Thank heaven it was Maureen. If someone had to see her like this, corpse colored, hair all over her face, she preferred it to be her mother. Exclaiming and sympathetic, Maureen helped her to her feet and supported her back to bed. Later she brought her a glass of water and a damp flannel for her face. "I bet it was that fish," she said tactlessly. "I wasn't too sure about it at the time."

"Please," moaned Molly, knowing without knowing how she knew that her affliction was the product of her struggle with the enemy in the mirror, but still unable to bear the thought of the meal she had eaten the night before. "I think it's just a bug," she managed to say. "Everyone's had it at school."

Floris was stirring, flinging up an arm. Molly remembered her terror as the little thin arm blurred, seemed to become pinioned, feathered. Something in her shrank from the memory. *It was a dream. Let it have been a dream.*

"I'll take him back to bed with me," whispered Maureen, bundling the surprised little boy up in her arms. He was flushed and rosy with sleep, his hair a disheveled cloud of honeysuckle gold. Waking, he clung instinctively to Maureen and she, her face a little swollen, as if she had been crying, put her lips gently to the damp curls. As she carried him out of the room she was lightly stroking his back in soothing, circular movements and murmuring to him words that Molly couldn't catch.

He looks so sweet but there's something wrong. There's something wrong with him. She feels sorry now but she was right. There's something worse than just not being able to talk. I just didn't want to see it.

But she felt nothing. Now that she was by herself, Molly lay like a stone. A narrow wand of sunlight moved slowly from the foot of her bed, traveling by degrees across her prone body until it lay directly, dazzling, across her face. But still she lay motionless, exhausted, emptied.

For most of the day she slept and woke only to, thankfully, sleep again. Once Maureen tiptoed in to say that she was going out and was Molly sure she'd be all right now on her own? Molly nodded, managing a smile, and fell back at once into the dream Maureen had interrupted in which an old lady was desperately trying to tell her something. This time there was a young woman with extraordinarily long hair and a restless impatient-seeming man with a pouncing hawklike face. They wanted to make her listen to some old story about two young lovers who died in a sacred place and whose grief was so dreadful that the great crystal that was

182

the Heartstone of the kingdom split as though struck by lightning and could never be mended because one piece— She couldn't concentrate at all. They seemed to be on the seashore. She could see the wind whipping their hair and hear the gulls crying. But she couldn't understand what they wanted from her. She was so tired. I'm too tired, she tried to tell them. I can't do anything for you now.

Then there was a woman with burning eyes, rocking and rocking, a little white bundle of baby clothes cradled in her arms. I'm too tired, Molly tried to tell her desperately. It's no use asking me. I'm just ordinary. You've made a mistake. Then the seashore vanished inexplicably and she found herself in a disturbingly dark room with walls that retreated from her as soon as she approached them. When she looked up she saw that there was no ceiling, only a stormy night sky crazed across again and again with forked lightning. She knew she was meant to ignore the storm and use the livid lightning flashes to help her with her task of putting together an enormous puzzle. But instead of real jigsaw puzzle pieces she had been given the sharp and shining fragments of stars and moons and planets that only she could fix back into their proper places. The pieces were cunning and slippery though, with minds of their own, and dodged about, eluding her. "This is impossible," she cried angrily. But at the very moment she cried out, she actually captured one and it flew across the room and turned into a child in a nightdress so worn and washed it was hard to say what its color was, but it reminded Molly of one Maureen had once made for her when she was little and which she had loved. The next piece she seized shimmered into a tired young woman in a nurse's uniform. She walked away from Molly smiling rather sadly and her smile was Maureen's smile. But the third piece actually struck Molly lightly on her hand and turned, laughing, into a shining, long-legged girl with red hair and a bright moon on her breast. Now, without her interference, one after another, the pieces sprang maddeningly into life. The room was thronging with small female children, half-grown girls and young women, who all looked as if they could be Molly's sisters. She was in despair. She would never get this puzzle finished. "I don't even know what it's meant to be when it's done," she wept, overwhelmed by these strange yet familiar people who all seemed to be speaking at once.

"Of course you do, silly," said Icarus, who had been sitting all this time in a small sunburst of light which had found its way, somehow, into the dark shifting spaces of this frightening room. And he pointed at the night sky over their heads and she saw, through the storm, that there was a vast black empty space where a constellation ought to be.

"Which one is it then?" begged Molly, still hopelessly confused. "I wish you'd tell me. I've got two star signs. Is it the Twins?"

"Oh, Molly, don't you know yet?" said Icarus affectionately. "It's as plain as the nose on your face—"

The light drained rapidly from the scene and she woke muttering and confused to find Sean lounging in the doorway saying something to her insistently.

"Oy," he said, as if for the umpteenth time. "Cloth-ears! *Moll.* Someone to see ya."

With great difficulty, she focused her eyes, trying to understand where she was and what day it might be. "Who?" she said, stupidly. "What did you say?"

"*I* don't know who he is, do I?" said Sean righteously. "Some hippy bloke. How should I know? Your boyfriend, I suppose. Tomkins or whatever he calls himself."

She shot up in her bed as though electrified and then clutched her reeling head. "Oh, Sean, get me my hairbrush. I must look awful."

"Don't know what Mum would say," he said, his face pulled into what he seemed to hope was a sneer. *"Secret admirers."* But he tossed her hairbrush in approximately her direction and sauntered out of her room with his new stiff-legged, sprung-heeled walk, copied from Vince, who had copied it from a jeans commercial he admired.

A few minutes later, Icarus peered around her door to find her trying uselessly to drag the brush through her matted hair with hands that were fluid and boneless as water.

"What have you been doing to yourself?" he said, concern flooding his face. "I go away for five minutes and look what happens. Here. Let me help." She was too weak to refuse. He sat on the bed, took the brush from her feeble hands and set to work, patiently, wordlessly, to get the tangles out. In the long silence there was too much that she wanted to say but couldn't. Her illness had left her vulnerable. If she spoke, she was afraid she would burst out crying. But so wildly knotted was her hair and so patiently thorough was Icarus, that by the time he had finished and ordered her to collapse onto her pillows, she felt more comfortable with him. She could even smile.

"I'd decided you were a dream," she said. "It's nice of you to visit me."

"I'd have come before," he said, transferring himself to the little armchair beside her bed and lowering himself cautiously onto the broken spring. "But my sister was having a bad time and my dad wanted me to go and stay with her for a while." He was looking very tired, Molly realized. He looks after people, like Maureen does, she thought. "Is she okay now?"

"Not really. She's gone back into this clinic where she goes sometimes. She'll only be there for a while." He stretched out his feet and gave her a lopsided attempt at a smile. She sensed his reluctance to say any more about his sister's troubles.

"What's her name?" asked Molly. "Is it mythical, like yours?"

"Cassandra," he supplied. "Cassandra Sky Tomkins. She gave me something for you." He felt around in his denim jacket and finally produced a small package from an inner pocket. He unwrapped a layer of tissue that released a sharp, sweet perfume and let something fall, smooth and bright, into her open hand. It was a moon badge. Sister to Floris's sun: a silvery crescent, enameled on a disc of wood. It was simple, yet oddly magical. She turned it over and found her name written on the back in tiny, flowing, silver letters.

When she could speak, she said, "I'll pin it on my coat."

"You were meant to," he said, nodding, pleased, seeing how much she liked it. "She said she hoped she'd meet you sometime. Anyway, Molly Gurney, what have you been doing to get yourself into this state?"

"I'm not sure," she said unhappily. "Icarus, really peculiar things have been happening. Scary things to do with Floris..." She stopped. He would think she was mad. "When I was ill I saw all kinds of things I couldn't really have seen," she said. She frowned. Her hand went to her face. She had a strange dizzy sensation. For a moment she was afraid the air would darken and glitter. She mustn't think about it or he... "I can't remember what I was saying," she said, confused. "Icarus, could you find your way down to the kitchen and make us some tea? Suddenly I'm really thirsty." *And I can't get warm,* she thought.

"Sure. Do you think I could grab a bit of bread while I'm there? I haven't eaten for a while. There's never a great deal to eat at Cassy's."

"Oh, you should have *said!*"

"Don't get all guilty and mortified. It's not important. Where's the little florist today? Out playing his penny whistle? Doing me out of business?"

She felt another pang of fear as she said, "Out

with Mum, I think." What had Maureen decided to do about Floris? The trouble was that now Molly wasn't sure what she *wanted* Maureen to do. There was something wrong with Floris. Something hidden and terrible. He wasn't what he seemed. He . . . Icarus was waiting patiently, and she dragged herself guiltily back to the present.

"If you like cheese," she said, smiling and trying to sound normal, "there should be some in the pantry. And there's usually a tomato or two in the fridge." He disappeared for a while and then came back, whistling something Celtic and plaintive, carrying a full tray.

"Who's the druid, by the way?" he asked, setting it down on her chest of drawers.

She was puzzled and then, light dawning, began to laugh weakly. "You must have seen Henry Preece in the Incredible Indigo Dressing-Gown. That's just what he looks like! I'll never be able to look at him with a straight face again."

"And the tough character in motorbike gear watching *Dangermouse* has to be one of your brothers?" She nodded. "I guess—Clifford." She nodded again and he gestured a vague triumphal gesture with an extremely ragged sandwich and began to eat hungrily. "What's the trouble with little Floris, then?" he asked, chewing. "Parents turned up or something?"

Molly shook her head. "He's been a bit…Maureen thinks he might actually be seriously disturbed. He bit another kid at playgroup."

"Well, the kid must have had it coming to him," pronounced Icarus staunchly. "Floris *disturbed*? He's an incredibly serene kid. I really like him. I'll never forget coming across him dancing like that in the middle of that hideous plastic piazza. I kept expecting Maid Marian to come on, you know. As if he was dancing in the heart of Sherwood Forest to some beautiful secret music."

"I know he seems sweet," said Molly, picking nervously at her bedcovers, "but lately I've started to think there *might* be something badly wrong with him. I've suddenly realized that I don't really know him at all. What he's really thinking, I mean." She didn't want them to talk about Floris anymore. At any moment the air might glitter and darken, the eggshell walls of her own world fall crashing inward, invaded, destroyed.

"Have you got to rush off and see anyone or anything?" she asked Icarus, hesitantly.

Icarus shook his head and started on his second sandwich. "No," he said. "So if you were going to invite me to stay to supper, I'd be delighted." He grinned at her out of his pale tired face, nearly the old grin. It was almost the way it had been between them. If only she didn't feel so frightened. If only she could keep everything apart: separate.

CHAPTER FIFTEEN

"The Change-Thinge of Launde"

Molly was miserable. No longer officially ill, she had been out of bed and up and around for a day or two now, able to eat a little, without enthusiasm it was true, and to sit on the sofa and watch television. But still she felt all wrong. Not exactly ill, but not as she had been before. Not Molly. And she couldn't keep warm, even huddled up to the heater and wearing the wonderful fluffy angora sweater Maureen had found her in an especially good rummage sale last winter. She should have been happy. After an initial suspicious maternal sniffing on Maureen's part, Icarus and her mother got on like a house on fire, and since that first supper Icarus had come round several times. She should have been happy. But she wasn't.

While Maureen and Icarus sat laughing and talking, Floris flitted like a pale silent changeling child from one to the other, gazing at their faces, smiling when they smiled, frowning when they frowned. Molly sat withdrawn, indifferent, as though behind some barrier of dark impervious glass. As though it was now she who watched from within the glittering darkness of the mirror and sneered at the unreality of all she saw.

Maureen had decided to give Floris the benefit of the doubt: her phrase. It meant she was ashamed of herself for being turned against a tiny child by "a load of narrowminded women," she said. She wouldn't respect their opinion on anything else, so why listen to what they thought about Floris when she lived with him and they didn't. She was going to send him to another playgroup in town. So what if it was a long bus ride? She would have done the same for one of her own.

Which is the real Maureen? Molly thought dully. The angry frightened one who was going to hand Floris over to some child shrink? Or this one who's so kind to everyone, spreading herself like thin healing ointment and leaving nothing for herself? And which is the real me? The ordinary one or the one who sees things that aren't— She shut off the thought. She had to keep things separate. It was the only way she could manage. It was— Floris stumbled over her foot as he ran past her chair, giggling at something Icarus had said. Instinctively he put out his hand to save himself by grasping Molly but she drew back as sharply as if he had struck at her. He fell, a puzzled expression on his face, but didn't cry, only slowly picked himself up and silently withdrew to stand by Maureen's chair. Responding unconsciously to his presence, Maureen put an arm around him and the little boy snuggled up to her like a puppy. *I don't think he ever loved me*. The realization made her shiver again. She pulled down the fleecy sleeves of her sweater so she could warm her blue hands inside the wristbands. *He'll cuddle up to anyone*. She had a sudden unwanted memory of Floris on the sofa next to Cliff, cradling that great motorcycle helmet in his small arms.

"I think it would do her good," Maureen was saying. "Don't you think so, Moll?" Molly shook her head to clear it, peering at her mother through the gathering fog in her head.

"What?"

"Icarus said perhaps he could take you out for a drive and a cup of tea somewhere. I think it would cheer you up."

"I don't mind," she said blankly.

Icarus looked almost hurt for a minute, she thought, but he was so quickly smiling at her again that she must have imagined it.

"Well, get your coat," prompted Maureen. "Floris will be all right in his jacket."

So he was coming too, was he? Well, so what? Icarus seemed to take more interest in him now than he did in her. Like a sleepwalker she went into the hall and fetched her coat but then just stood passively waiting with the coat folded over her arm.

"It *is* quite warm once you're out," said Icarus, as if he was apologizing for her, Molly thought, irritated.

"Then I'll leave it," she said. Nothing kept her warm anyway. So what if she caught a chill? If she died of pneumonia she couldn't care less, she thought. Then a surviving spark of the old Molly flared into brief life. What's happening to me? *A splinter of ice* . . .

Outdoors she took great lungfuls of air, hoping it would make her feel better. It did seem to clear her head a little. She gave Icarus a wan smile and climbed into the car.

"Where do you want to go?" he asked.

"Anywhere. I don't know. The moors maybe?"

she said, struggling against the terrible indifference that seemed to be weighing her down like great pocketfuls of old snow.

She didn't know how long they drove. The scenery wound past them like a film. Remote, disconnected from her. A soft sunlit sky the color of harebells: miles of stone wall and miles of golden gorse and pink-and-white heather. Icarus wound down Tin Witch's window so she could smell the honey fragrance and hear the larks singing, but she began to shiver so violently that he wound it back up again almost at once. He tried to talk to her several times but she kept hearing herself answering in that hatefully cold hostile voice and after a while he left her alone and talked to Floris instead.

The Magus was looking for her. She knew it as clearly as if he had spoken directly into her mind. He was reaching out for her. It was as if she were on the end of his line and he was reeling her in, tighter, closer, tighter and closer, always with that look of chilling contempt, that drowning emptiness in his eyes. *He's put a splinter of ice in* . . . What did she mean? What was that story? The fog in her head was growing thicker. Dimly she heard Icarus say, "Molly, shall we go home? Don't you feel well?"

They were away from the moors now, driving down a busy main road. Molly saw the outline of the large industrial estate looming up ahead. They were passing a roadhouse, a luridly decorated wayside café of the kind she had always loathed. To advertise it, someone had suspended a gigantic hot air balloon, painted to look like an insanely grinning fried egg. It would be full of people in there. People and noise and the smell of fried food. Perhaps even a juke box. He wouldn't dare to come for her in there.

"Let's go in there," she said loudly, to reach him through the roaring fog in her head. "Let's have a cup of tea in there."

"You're *kidding*," said Icarus, his jaw dropping. I loathe those places. I bet you do too."

"Oh, come on," she said desperately, trying to smile and be animated. "It'll be fun."

He stared at her for a moment and then shrugged. "Okay. If that's what you want."

She couldn't bear the bewilderment in his face as he reversed the car some few hundred meters and parked in the car park of the roadhouse. Before they went in, Icarus made one last attempt to reach her. As she was trying to open her door he put his hand on her arm and said pleadingly, "Moll—" But she pulled away as if she hadn't noticed, dragged Floris roughly out of the back of the car and, gripping his hand tightly, walked so fast toward the café that the little boy began to whimper with fear and pain.

Icarus caught up with them and lifted Floris into his arms. "You're running him off his legs," he said angrily. "Whatever's got into you?"

Still ignoring him, she opened the door and walked gratefully into a wall of noise. *We'll be safe in here.* If only she could see through the fog. Silent with dislike of her now, Icarus found them a table and went to the counter to order them something to drink. *After this I'll never see him again.* She felt nothing anymore except that relief people are said to feel when they lie down in a snowdrift to die.

When Icarus came back, Floris climbed onto his knee and leaned back against him confidingly, gazing up into his face. He was being his sweetest, most charming, most pliant small self and Molly felt a cold violent surge of hatred for him. *Who is he after all? He hasn't any personality of his own. He's just a sort of empty mirror, reflecting back anything that looks into it.*

This thought frightened her. Something in her bones tried to warn her that it could do terrible damage. She began to feel dizzy. Panicky. It was no good. The fog seemed to be spreading all around. She had thought they would be safe in here, amongst the noisy crowd. But still the Magus was winding her closer and closer. She felt so weak, so ill. She looked up, trying to make her numb lips move. She wanted to tell Icarus he must take her home. But there was a dark buzzing between herself and Icarus that scared her. Looking round, she dimly saw people at a remote distance laughing and talking. But she was only half here. She had lurched by terrible mistake into this in-between place which only she could see and hear. Icarus was turned toward her, his face alarmed, but he too seemed frozen, suspended, far away.

And the Magus was standing over her, triumphant. With his hooded, reptilian gaze he had watched her from within her own mirror. Trembling, she drew back from the famished darkness that waited in those eyes. She recognized their devouring despair as kin to the icy darkness that had been gathering in her own heart.

"I didn't mean..." she faltered, her lips stiff.

"No. You were right," he said. "And now you know the truth, you will let him go. Now you understand what manner of thing you have been harboring, you will let him go. A long, long tedious time we have had, trying to draw him back to us that he might be penned in his proper style— but your mistaken *love*, as I suppose you thought of it, formed a resistant barrier most wearing to

penetrate. Until we *helped* you to see the truth—
Let go of him!" For she had reached for Floris
unconsciously. Somehow he was standing beside her
in this cold, strange nowhere place, and she clung
to his small warm hand with her trembling cold
one. The dark air bore down upon them oppres-
sively like a blizzard of furious bees.

"He's only a little boy," she whispered, her lips
barely moving. The scorn of the Magus vibrated
through the stinging air like an arctic frost. He
reached out and grasped Floris by his free hand and
wrenched him out of her grip, his face contorting.

"*This!*" he almost spat. "You have been misled
and bemused by hedge wizards and outcasts and
deranged old women. Shall I show you *what* this
is?"

Floris was shrinking back, terrified of this raging
figure who towered threateningly over them. Then
he began to blur and change.

Before her horrified eyes, his outline fuzzed. His
delicate face blunted and thrust out a dark whiskery
muzzle. His eyes became wild, yellow, inhuman.
His body sprouted rough hair, gray as gunmetal,
stooped and dropped onto all fours, whimpering
and shivering, and it was finished. A cringing wolf
cub put up its snout and began to howl like a
desolate puppy.

"That is no *child!*" cried the Magus of Harper's Ford, his voice bitter with disgust. "It is *the Change-Thinge of Launde* and I take it at last to the place the Law has appointed."

The buzzing in the air intensified to a roaring glitter. Too late, weeping, she reached for the frantic little beast, to take it in her arms, to protect it and comfort it. But a freezing wind hurled her backward. There was a rushing of air and blackness.

CHAPTER SIXTEEN

Lost

She came round to find herself on the back seat of the Tin Witch. Icarus was bending over her, his face greenish with shock. Then it all flooded back to her and she began to sob at the memory of what she had done. Her horror at the hideous transformation of her little foster brother was nothing compared to the horror she felt at her own failure. Again and again she heard the loathing in the Magus's voice, again and again saw his gloating face. She reached out wordlessly for Icarus and without hesitation he put his arms round her. But as she sobbed hopelessly into his shoulder she heard him say: "Don't you think you might tell me what's going on now, Molly?"

She began to wail like a five-year-old that he would never understand, would never believe her in a thousand years, but he silenced her: "I saw enough in there, Molly. Don't tell me what I will or won't believe. And I saw—what he did to Floris."

She felt him trembling against her and after a while he pulled away from her, dashing a hand over his eyes. "At least you're looking like Molly Gurney again," he said shakily, trying to grin at her. "You were so scary before, Moll. Blank and frozen. As if you were under a spell. No—no, we haven't got the time for you to do this," he said, hushing her as she started to sob even more violently. "Later we'll both have a good cry about it, but just now I think you should tell me who that bastard is we're dealing with."

And so, halting, hiccupping, she began at last to try to piece for Icarus and herself all the broken fragments together. Now that the worst had happened and she had lost Floris to the enemy, there was no longer any reason to keep it all separate.

"So what are you telling me then?" Icarus demanded incredulously. "That that beautiful sensitive little kid is really a *werewolf* or something? This

Lord Thingy's seventh child turns out to be under the Curse of the Werewolf?"

"No, I don't think so," said Molly, still having to sniff hard. "I know that's what he made it look like. I think he did that—horrible thing to convince me finally that Floris wasn't a human child so I'd let him go.... But he called him a 'Change-Thinge.' I think that means Floris can't help being changed by people's thoughts. I was just beginning to realize it myself, but I didn't properly understand. *They* seem to think it's some sort of family curse. Something that just crops up every now and then every generation or so in Floris's family. Lady Agnes and the moody man in the tower were talking about it. Lady Agnes is sure the Magus's family is to blame because they've always been an evil lot and because hundreds of years ago one of Floris's ancestors—I think he was called Dominis—fell in love with the Lord of Harper's daughter. I'm not sure if the Lord was a Magus then or if he sort of became one later. Anyway they were forbidden to marry, so they chose to die instead and ever since then the kingdom has been cursed, apparently because some old stone was broken."

"But Floris's family got cursed worst of all. It sounds as if the Magus is keeping it going, then, doesn't it?"

"I don't know," said Molly doubtfully. "The Keeper didn't seem to—" She stopped for a minute and then said slowly: "I've been learning about it *all the time*, but I kept telling myself it was only imagination. Or only dreams. Or else I didn't remember the dreams once I woke up. But now it's all coming together and I don't understand why I couldn't see it before. Oh, Icarus, I've been so stupid. And such a coward." Her eyes filled with tears again. "If I hadn't . . . When he first came"—she was fighting to control her voice—"Maureen said he was covered with bruises. The worst she'd ever seen, she said. But in the morning I couldn't find any. Not a single one. She expected to see them, you see. She's always so upset when we get hurt children. . . . She always reads all the awful stories in the newspaper and cries over them and feels guilty because she can't foster a thousand unwanted children. And my father, you see . . . And I was missing Wayne a lot. I was just getting to know him when he went back to the family that had hurt him so badly in the first place. And so Floris sort of replaced him for me— even his little gestures. . . . He couldn't help doing it. He just can't help tuning in to people's really powerful important thoughts and becoming what's in their minds. But isn't that awful, Icarus—it means no one ever really knows Floris, only what he seems to be when he's with them. He must be the loneliest—But when *we* changed him, it happened by accident. The Magus knows how to use it. . . . But—oh, Icarus, that must have been why he bit that awful aggressive little boy at playgroup. . . ."

She struggled up in her seat. "Icarus, if you don't hate me too much, could you please drive me somewhere? I've got to try to reach the Keepers, the visitors." Had she only just realized that they were one and the same? Her everyday world and the elusive shadow world of her dreams slid suddenly one into the other, making one luminous whole instead of two split and unfinished realities. "It's the only place I can think of to try."

"Of course I'll drive you, idiot. Don't you think I want to help you get Floris back from that—that *death's head!*" She had never imagined Icarus could be so angry, so upset. Then he said in a very determined way, "And of course I don't hate you. We had our lines crossed, that's all. You didn't trust me enough to tell me what was frightening you. I wish you had."

"Oh, Icarus, however shall we get him back? And what will I tell Mum?"

She wept quietly beside him in Tin Witch all the way to the corner of Rustling Lane where the SOLD sign had just been nailed up outside Albert

Villas. At any other time she would have laughed outright at the astonished expression on Icarus's face as he took in the respectable Victorian semi-detached stone houses, each with a stained-glass panel over its front door, and said, "What? Here?"

"It's hard to explain," said Molly. "The world he comes from—it isn't in some separate place. It sort of overlaps with ours. We just haven't learned how to see it. I think it might be like wavelengths—you have to tune in. I can only do it by accident so far. The house with the octagonal tower, in my dream: I've been able to see it here sometimes. I don't remember when it started. I know it sounds really crazy," she said apologetically. And then she was out of the car, running up the path to the empty house.

But I know it's no good. I can't see it. It isn't just that I can't see it. I can't feel it. They've shut me out. Because I failed—because I betrayed them.

Tears were running down her swollen face. They fell indifferently like rain and she no longer noticed them but ran frantically to the back of the house where the previous owners had left large quantities of rubbish tied up in black plastic garbage bags. There was a roll of old threadbare carpet and a dirty rabbit hutch, all waiting for the sanitation workers to take them away. She stared around wildly.

I know it's here. *I just have to find the wavelength and tune in.* Nothing. Nothing. The empty air mocked her.

She peered in first the kitchen and then the dining room windows: bare floorboards silted with dust. Old-fashioned wallpaper discolored in random squares and oblongs where pictures or mirrors had hung. Damp patches. A wooden cotton reel that had rolled into a corner unnoticed: Molly could see the few strands of sky-blue thread left on it. Just an ordinary, empty, rather neglected old house. It had been her last futile hope.

She went back to the car with a face so starkly forlorn that there was no need for her to say anything. Icarus started the engine as soon as she got in.

"But where are we going?" she demanded in pure terror. "I can't go home."

"My aunt Dorothy's," said Icarus simply. And that's all he would say.

CHAPTER SEVENTEEN

Alias Tamara

Icarus's aunt Dorothy drew the curtains, which were thick and also lined with heavy, dark, draft-excluding material so that the room at once became intensely dark and shadowy, yet sharply focused on the honey-gold circle of candlelight. Simultaneously it fell silent with a hushed silence, disturbingly like a third presence.

Molly was acutely uncomfortable. Her hands sweated. Dorothy, alias Tamara, alias Icarus's aunt, lived in a hideous nineteen-thirties bungalow at the end of a bumpy, unpaved road in a backwater of Bradley quite new to her. The house, at least from the outside, was so unlike its owner that she felt confused. It was a sentimental fake of a cottage, incorporating all periods but belonging to none: so elaborately overdecorated with mock Tudor mullions, stained-glass portholes, barley-sugar twists of this and little carved curlicues of that, and even the occasional Alpine shutter, that it could have been a film set from a very old, very bad Hollywood film. Waiting for the door to open she found herself absently touching the little panes of colored glass to see if they were sticky.

"The Gingerbread House," whispered Icarus, catching her at it. "Incredible, isn't it?"

But Dorothy herself had been putting finishing touches to some clay pots in a chaotic-looking studio attached to the back of the house when Molly and Icarus arrived. She was not wearing fussy flowery clothes and shawls and dangling earrings but spattered and disreputable potter's jeans. She was small and rather fierce with a wiry crop of silvering dark curly hair. Her blue eyes were very blue and took in everything she seemed to need to know about them when they burst in on her, almost in-incoherent with distress, but she wouldn't let them explain anything until she'd sat Molly and Icarus down to drink a calming cup of strong tea. It wasn't even herb tea.

But now she had at least changed into a clean

sweater of fine black wool. In the dark clothing her body dissolved into the shadow. Her face and hands became at once more vivid and more mysterious. But when she spoke it was in the same throaty and humorous common-sense tones she had used to Molly before.

"Strictly speaking, we don't need all this," she said, as Molly took in the objects on the covered table. "But it isn't bogus either. It will help to concentrate the mind. Here are all the four elements. Fire and air"—She gestured slightly at the tall white candles whose flames wavered for a second. "Water." She touched a blue pottery jug and lifted it. "And this bowl"—she poured water in a swift bright stream from the jug—"is made of crystal which is of the earth—even though it looks such an extraordinarily starry thing now."

Molly moved closer, reluctantly drawn by the candlelit water in this beautiful glimmering bowl that seemed to float now in the dark ocean of the room.

"The thing about crystal," said Dorothy, in the same down-to-earth manner she had used earlier to explain the idiosyncrasies of her kiln, "is that it is astonishingly powerful stuff. And different crystals have different qualities in much the same way that people have different personalities and different talents. But they also share certain common qualities. Crystals, that is. Since ancient times people in our world have known this intuitively. Some people." She glanced across at Molly who was clearly embarrassed and stifling a yawn, and she grinned, quite unabashed. "No, duck. It's not hocus-pocus. It's perfectly true. But all you need to know for now is that crystal acts as an intermediary between worlds or dimensions—or whatever word you want to use. You don't *have* to have it, of course, but it steps up the— What's the matter, duckling?" For Molly had sat down abruptly on the arm of a chair as if all the air had been knocked out of her.

"Nothing," she said hoarsely. "But in my dream of the tower, the octagonal room—there were hundreds of different crystals in it. I got the impression—I think I did—that the man, the Keeper, worked with them in some way."

Dorothy looked at her keenly. "Well, now. We'll have to see what else you can remember later. But it looks as if you've learned how to dream between the worlds. It does happen. And you had the little boy as a link, which— Oh, my dear!"

Molly's hands had flown to her face and she was weeping. "I'm sorry, I'm sorry," she gasped. "But they trusted me and I lost him and it was all my fault. If I hadn't got so frightened—if I could just undo it all—"

Dorothy did not take Molly in her arms and mother or comfort her. She didn't even change the tone of her voice when she spoke to her. Alarmingly, she spoke to her as if she were another grown-up. "If you were able to undo it all, you would never have learned what you know now, would you? You would have it all still to go through at some time or another. Molly, guilt is a complete waste of time and energy, believe me. It can waste whole lifetimes. What we can change we must try to change, put right. But everything else—we just have to learn to live with."

Molly looked up. Dorothy was not just using words on her the way adults so often did. She was saying what she really knew. Shuddering with the effort to keep back her tears, she said, blinking: "I'm sorry. Let's get on with it, whatever it is. Please may we?" She stood up again and then Dorothy did reach across the table, the candles flaming between them, and touched her shoulder briefly as though she approved of her.

"Right, dear," she said. "All I want you to do is to sit with me here in this room, quietly, and think about this little boy. Think about the times you had with him, especially the good times. Fill yourself with thoughts and memories of him until he is clearly and powerfully present in your mind. We are using your love for him, your bond with him, to reach him through the crystal. It isn't witchcraft, you know. The crystal is just by its nature a super-sensitive medium, a living, conscious medium, as live as you are. It will respond to the power and direction of your thoughts and focus them for you. It just intensifies the power that is already present: amplifies it. But it's *your* thoughts and intentions that are the source of the power. Your love for Floris. Do you understand?"

Molly nodded. She pulled a chair up to the table so that she was sitting opposite Dorothy, and by some instinct placed her hands on the crystal bowl, close to but not touching Dorothy's small dry hands with their broken nails. Instantly she felt a tingling current, a surge of energy, and knew that it flowed from Dorothy. "You have a knack for this sort of thing obviously," said Dorothy softly, almost affectionately. "Now fill your mind..."

They sat in silence for a long, long time.

After a while something of the quality of a dream stole around them. Things seemed less solid. The darkness seemed to ebb and flow in subtle tides. The silence, too, played tricks: shrinking and expanding, roaring in Molly's ears like ocean waves and then vanishing into nothing but the sound of her own blood moving in her veins.

Then Molly thought some draft in the room had altered the reflection of the candles in the water, for something had changed in it, though whether shape or color or intensity she couldn't tell. The tingling in her hands increased until it was an uncomfortably hot buzzing, and the old voices in her bones, which had been whispering ever since she first entered the room, burst forth into irrepressible song.

She was dimly aware of Dorothy giving her an odd look but was too deeply involved in the disturbed rainbow dancing in the water to pay real attention. Rivers of light flowed through her fingers, rivers of light. She could become like the river, she could let go of something in herself and slide in—she could . . .

"I can see him," she whispered, the blood draining from her face. Her voice came from far away. Her voice was speaking, not her.

"I can sense him," murmured Dorothy, "poor mite. But not see him. Describe where he is."

Molly was shivering: "It's so cold. A cold, freezing place. You know those special rooms where butchers hang the meat—the carcasses? That's how it feels. But it glitters. It's made out of crystal like this bowl and it glitters all over like icy fire. It's some kind of crystal maze or labyrinth underground, and the place where they've put him is at the center of it. They're afraid of him. I didn't understand that before. They've put him here because here he can't—change, for some reason. The curse doesn't work or something." Her teeth were chattering. "He's all on his own, Dorothy. He's lying on the hard glittering ground, without even a blanket. And it's as white and cold as the inside of the moon. He's in his own shape—like a little boy, I mean, and I think he's in some kind of drugged sleep. He's all curled up the way babies are before they're born."

"It isn't a natural sleep, you're right," said Dorothy, barely audibly. "It's some very crude but powerful drug. It simulates something very close to death. His heartbeat is very faint. His blood is very slow."

"He's so afraid," said Molly. "Even in his dreams he's afraid. He's calling and calling out in his dream but no sound will come, no one can see how hard he's trying to call to them. And now he's trying to run and run but nothing moves, everything stays frozen in the same place and so does he, his legs can't carry him and he's been afraid like this for almost his whole—except..."

"He's dreaming of you now," whispered Dorothy.

"Your thoughts are reaching him, they're so strong and loving...."

In the fiery frame of the candlelit water, Molly saw the little boy in his dirty rummage-sale jeans and his TOUGH GUY jacket pinned with the small lion-haired sun. Almost imperceptibly he was uncurling, slowly thawing out of his frozen fetal huddle. A faint wistful smile flickered briefly over his small, white, pointed face. The jewel in his ear was pulsing rose, lavender, violet.

"I love you," she said silently. "I do love you. We'll get you back home safe, little one. Don't be afraid. Don't give up. We'll find a way." Her tears blinded her. When she had blinked them furiously back, all she could see in the crystal bowl were the scattered and broken reflections of tongues of candleflame.

"He's gone," said Dorothy. "He's gone now." She sat back in her chair looking very tired suddenly. "But you did so well, duckling. You got through. You reached him."

"But I'm the one who *lost* him—if it hadn't been for me . . ." Molly blew her nose, blinded again, and speechless for a moment at the enormity of what Floris had meant to her, what she had thrown away. She would never forgive herself as long as she lived. Whatever Dorothy said, she knew herself to be a terrible person and there was no way she could undo this appalling self-knowledge.

Dorothy sat in silence for a while, seeming to be very deep in thought. Then she got up. "I'll tell you what I think," she said, pulling back the curtains with some difficulty, for they were long and heavy and she was fairly small. Molly waited, apprehensive, for revelation.

Evening light slipped softly into the room. Over the rooftops was a single star. The last glow of sunset was dimming through final hazes of lavender and violet to a deep, swimming, mysterious green-blue.

"I think," announced Dorothy, "that there's some homemade pizza in my freezer. One of my better ones, with black olives *and* mozzarella cheese. And I know there's a huge pot of onion soup and some good bread because Icarus helped me to make it earlier today. Let's go and eat. Why, what's the matter, duckling? Have I said something indecent?" She chuckled, seeming not at all put out that Molly was glaring at her and even clenching her hands as though she wanted to hit her.

"I *thought* we were trying to find my foster brother," spluttered Molly in total furious confusion. "I *thought* you promised to help. We've both just seen him almost *dying* in that awful ice labyrinth, all frightened and alone. And *you* say: 'Let's have supper.' And what have you got lined up for after supper—*tickets for the Bradley Playhouse?*" Her voice was as withering as she could make it.

Dorothy laughed outright. "When did you last eat?"

Molly scowled. "I don't know. Lunchtime I suppose. No, I was feeling terrible then so I didn't. It must have been breakfast then. Oh, except there wasn't any bread and Floris had the last of the cereal...but I still—"

"And when will you eat next?"

"I don't—"

"Precisely," said Dorothy triumphantly. "And if my bones tell me right, this is going to be one of the longest, hardest nights you'll ever experience. So you'll need something to put the stomach back into you. Also the kind of work we've been doing is really very taxing—"

Molly had just found this out for herself, struggling to stay upright on legs that had turned suddenly to marshmallow.

"Furthermore"—Dorothy's eyes were twinkling away—"I'm the kind of irritating person who can never see the answer if they're staring too hard at the question. I see most clearly out of the farthest corner of my eye."

"Oh I see," said Molly, suddenly liking Icarus's aunt very much. "Yes I see. Yes, so do I, I think. I am sorry for being rude and whining—"

"Perfectly understandable," Dorothy interrupted cheerfully, leading the way back to her beautiful kitchen. "Oh, Icarus, you dear thing, you've read my mind and put the pizza in the oven already."

It was the nicest supper Molly had ever eaten, sitting at the old-fashioned farmhouse table beside Icarus and across from his aunt Dorothy: the new moon and a trio of stars framed in the uncurtained window, creamy petals spilling onto a blue cloth from a jug of old-fashioned roses. How could she feel so safe and happy in the very middle of such a horrible and frightening experience?

They sat amidst the wreckage of the meal for a long while, drinking coffee and eating sweet dark cherries, the first Molly had eaten that summer.

"Earrings for you," said Icarus softly, hanging a twinned cherry over her ear.

"Twit," she said, going pink, recovering them and eating them swiftly.

Dorothy was gazing at them both as if she had all at once gone far off into another country and they were receding. Molly guessed she had suddenly seen something extremely clearly out of the farthest corner of her bright-blue eyes. But all she said was, "Molly, we must phone your mother and tell her you and Floris are staying the night. Icarus has brought you here to meet me and, lo and behold, here is his sister on a surprise visit with other small relatives who love Floris on sight. You are all getting on like a house on fire. It's such a shame to break up the party and Icarus's shockingly tolerant auntie says she loves to have her house full of noisy young people. That gives us the rest of the night to get him back and with any luck she may never need to know about him vanishing from the face of the earth."

"But I can't tell her a lie," panicked Molly. How could she explain to anyone else the way her mother often walked around in her head as though it was just another room in the Gurneys' house, a room that could always be let out if the need arose.

"Of course not, sweetie. *I* will. Gurney, isn't it? Is it in the book?"

"Yes, Vine Street," said Molly, her mouth dry. Dorothy rose and went into the hall, where Molly supposed the telephone to be, but she peered round the door again briefly to say, "It isn't strictly a lie, duckling. Look on it more as a piece of theater in a good cause."

So she wouldn't be able to hear so much as a murmur of this untruthful explanation—the very

thought of it made her break into a cold sweat—
Molly began to clear the table and wash the dishes.
Her unhappiness and anxiety had returned in a flood.
What had she got herself into? Deceiving her mother?
Putting her trust in some eccentric—perhaps batty—
old woman who was obviously dabbling in witch-
craft, whatever *she* might call it.

"The gods are on our side, anyway," said Dorothy,
beaming, coming back in. "Your mother had only
just got back from coping with some neighbor-
hood crisis. I told her we'd been phoning and phoning to let her know you were both safe and she
was very pleased, Molly, that you were having such
a nice time. She said it would do you good."

"But what do we tell her tomorrow," said Molly,
full of doom. "If—"

"Can you find me the street map of Bradley,
Ick?" Dorothy interrupted briskly. "We'd better get
a move on." He fetched it and she spread it Out on
the kitchen table and then produced something from
the pocket of her clay-streaked jeans. "Do leave the
dishes, Molly," she said. "I can do those after you've
gone."

Why? Where am I going? thought Molly, alarmed,
drying her hands.

"You might tell us what we're doing, Auntie Dot,"

said Icarus plaintively. "I feel as though I'm just about to be parachuted over enemy lines."

"Very intuitive of you," said Dorothy, dryly. "Exactly what I had in mind."

"I hope you 'ave brought your beret," murmured Icarus to Molly, who was grinning despite herself, "so the other members of the Resistance will recognize you, ma cherie."

Dorothy freed the object she had been holding in her hand: it swung gently on the end of a fine gold chain, a crystal in the shape of a teardrop. "Correspondences," she said. "We're looking for correspondences. Molly's said herself that the world Floris is from isn't in some other *place*. It's all around us if we only knew how to tune into it. Generally I use a pendulum for helping me to find things or people in this world. But I don't see why it couldn't help us find someone in another world. Somewhere in or near this town is a place that corresponds to that ice maze or labyrinth where they've put him."

So this was what she saw, shining out of the farthest corner of her fierce blue eye.

They stood silently as, the golden chain looped carefully over her fingers, Dorothy dangled the crystal pendulum first over one section of the map and then another. As the moments passed and the crystal remained motionless, Molly began to feel sick with disappointment and self-disgust. Why was she participating in this charade? How could she have been so gullible as to think such a batty idea would work? But just as she was about to blurt out something, anything, to break the dreadful tension building up inside her, the crystal suddenly began to revolve in great widening circles.

Molly found she couldn't breathe properly and Icarus, too, unconsciously clutched at her hand. "What have you got?" he said huskily. "Where is it, Dot?"

Dorothy peered at the map, tracing with her finger the radius of the agitated crystal. "Oh dear," she said mildly. "This really is a very old map, isn't it? The spot it's showing us on this map is the area where they knocked down almost a whole street about fifteen years ago: the old Glory Hallelujah Inn and all those funny shabby little shops and old warehouses down by the river. You won't remember, Icarus. There was a pet shop with canaries singing in the doorway and a shoe mender's and—"

"Molly's going psychic," said Icarus. "She gets that look when—"

"I know where it is," Molly said, very quietly, very frightened. "And I know what they built in its place—a gigantic multistory car park. It's the nearest thing Bradley's got to a labyrinth anyway."

The three of them stood in silence for a moment. Then Molly said bleakly, "Well, I'd better go then."

"What's all this 'I,'" demanded Icarus. "We both go. Or else no one goes."

"But it's my fault that we lost him. I'm the one who promised to take care of him. And the Magus—the man who's got him, he's really dangerous. I think he's gone mad with hating for so long. Why should you get hurt, Icarus?" she said, trembling.

She was terrified. But she had to go.

"You will both go," said Dorothy firmly. "Don't ask me how I know it, but I know Icarus is as important as you are in this, Molly. Moll—you'd better borrow my jacket. Waiting at night is cold work. And you'll need something for the little boy. A blanket to wrap him in. Icarus can get them and I'll make you up a thermos to take with you."

"Do we actually know what we're going to be doing?" asked Icarus, his voice muffled with his head in the coat cupboard. "I mean," he said, more distinctly, emerging, "do you have some kind of sheet music for us to follow, Dot, or will we just have to improvise brilliantly as we go along?"

"It'll come to you," said Dorothy, pushing them both toward the door. "Molly will know. You just need your hearts and your wits. If they fight you with ice, fight with fire. If they use their hate against you—use your love to turn it away. When you come down to it, it's the only energy in the universe. All the rest is a twisting and warping—whoever was that dreadful man who answered the phone to me, though, Moll?" she asked without drawing breath. "Is that your mother's lodger? She should get rid of him. He's the sort who couldn't stand to see anything run free. He'd have to hunt it down, lock it up and label it. Even his voice made me feel quite ill."

"He does me," agreed Molly, half in and half out of the door. "He wants Mum to marry."

"The druid?" asked Icarus, appalled. "Heaven forbid. Okay, Aunt Dorothy, we're going, honestly."

"You'll be quite safe in the car," Dorothy called after them.

Molly looked back at her, framed in the bright doorway of her Gingerbread House, a small, elderly woman radiating energy, the silver threads in her dark wiry curls glinting in the light, the white clay plastered all over her jeans, her sturdy independence endearingly obvious even from this distance.

"Why will we be safe in the car?" she whispered, giggling a little from sheer fear as Icarus fumbled for the keys to Green Tin Witch.

"Because," he said, with obvious embarrassment,

"she's put a circle of protection round it. She doesn't much trust the driving skills of adolescent males."

"Does it work?" She slid in through the car door, shivering, and began to grope for the seatbelt which in Tin Witch slithered in serpentine coils to the floor, tangling itself around the bottom of the seat.

"So far."

"Oh," said Molly, startled. "I can actually see it." As the Morris began to lumber along the unlit, unpaved road that led from Aunt Dorothy's house, she could see a moony shimmer enclosing the whole car like a luminous skin.

"Yes," said Icarus without surprise. "I can see it sometimes, too. Comforting, isn't it?"

CHAPTER EIGHTEEN

A Bridge of Moonlight

"I've always hated this place," said Molly as Tin Witch eased onto the first ramp of the multistory in pitch darkness. "It's worse than the ghost train at the November Fair. Smells worse, anyway. I bet the Glory Hallelujah Inn was much nicer than a Glory Hallelujah car park."

As they turned a corner, BRADLEY WANDERERS, in white spray-painted letters, flared at them in the headlights and then vanished.

"Where do we go?" asked Icarus. "Do you think it matters much?"

"Up another flight," she said. "At least—I don't know, Icarus. It's all so crazy. It's so unreal. I can't believe we're actually doing this. How can we possibly save him like this? I can't get my mind round it."

"You're going to have to start believing in the music in your own head one of these days," said Icarus quite sternly. "And when you do, there'll be no stopping you. You'll dazzle us all. Molly's comet!"

She stared at what she could see of his face in the dark beside her as the Morris bumped and lurched around corners. She thought he might have just said something important. But she only said, in the interests of accuracy, "It's in my bones, as a matter of fact, not in my head. This'll do, Icarus. Park up here somewhere."

He parked. "Then what?" he said.

"We wait," said Molly. "And we try to fill our minds with thoughts of Floris, like I did with Dorothy."

So for some embarrassing moments they sat, trying to ignore the cold and the tense sounds of their own breathing in the parked car, in the eerie darkness of a deserted car park.

"Not the best atmosphere really, is it?" said Icarus after a while in a rather apologetic voice.

"No," she agreed forlornly, wishing that he didn't seem to be looking to her all the time for advice and reassurance about what to do next. Dorothy had said Icarus was important, as important as—

Then it burst upon her with dazzling clarity. "Play, Icarus," she commanded. "Play to Floris—your tune, your special tune. He loves music, remember? He can't resist it, it's even stronger than the spell. Play for him!"

Startled, but instantly comprehending, he drew out the battered tin whistle. Molly opened the door. And Icarus began to play.

At first it had a frail, isolated sound to it, painfully lonely. Icarus was desperately nervous. Once he stopped to shake the spit out of his flute and said, trying to smile, "I've played some horrible gigs in my time, but this—"

But after a while Molly realized that one of the notes was vibrating more strongly than the others and lingered, warm and sweet as wild honey in the stagnant air, remaining to accompany the next notes Icarus was playing. And the next. The music was building in layers: an orchestral, almost tangible structure of sound as if a thousand flutists were emerging from the shadows and playing with all their hearts for Floris.

"It's your own tone," she whispered. "Your own true tone, Icarus. You're building a bridge between the worlds."

And all the time he was playing she thought of Floris, sending out her own strong certainty of her love for him, whoever or whatever he might be, like an inner song. As the moments passed, this inner song grew louder and louder rising from her bones, from her very cells, until it burst into her mind like light, a soundless, fierce, powerful summons.

Any door. Any door that you choose.

Her eye traveled to an upper doorway. *That one,* she said silently. Slowly, slowly the door she had chosen acquired a frail frame of light. Slowly, slowly the door moved outward: an inch or two. Icarus saw and his eyes widened but he didn't stop playing for a moment. The door was opening. They sang to it, she and Icarus, they called to it together, called and cajoled, besought it to open wider and wider until they were both trembling in every limb with the effort. The lettering on the door said FIRE EXIT. But the frame of the open doorway glittered with a crystalline ring of ice, like a door into the inside of the moon.

Keep playing, she told Icarus, beginning to climb out of Tin Witch. She barely realized she hadn't spoken aloud. Icarus looked alarmed but scrambled out of his own door, still playing.

Floris. Floris, she called silently.

And after an agonizing pause in which she could count her heartbeats—she saw him.

White as milk, dazed and blind as a sleepwalker, he came toward them, not down the steps of cement and steel in their reality, but stumbling uncertainly onto the frail impossible bridge of light and sound that Molly and Icarus had made. As he took his first tottering steps, it swayed sickeningly like a rope bridge in an Indiana Jones movie, but he did not look down or falter. As he drew closer and closer to the source of the flute music, a faint smile appeared on his small white face: They were drawing him deeper and deeper into the circle of sound, deeper and deeper into their world. He began to walk more confidently and then to trot, almost run. Now he was flying down the magic bridge, his arms held out.

"Floris!" called Molly in joy and fear. "Floris!" She had called out loud. He froze. A tremor crossed his face. He looked around, utterly bewildered, the spell broken. He looked down and, seeing nothing between his feet and a sickening drop into space but fragile filaments of moonlight, opened his mouth in a silent scream of terror.

Molly plunged forward, but as she did so, several threatening figures appeared in the doorway behind Floris, and simultaneously, as though a spotlight had been switched on in a theater, a second group of figures appeared on the opposite side of the car park in a shimmer of white.

"You shan't have him," Molly screamed. "I love him!" And caught him as he fell from the bridge, whimpering. She staggered under the impact. He was cold as death.

"Back to the car!" Icarus yelled, as if she needed telling. "Or they'll get him back again."

She began to run, but her body would not obey properly. It was like the running she remembered in dreams: Her legs pounding in futile slow motion across the short distance to Tin Witch, the space between herself and safety never growing less, the ice-cold child in her arms growing heavier and heavier at every step.

Then she realized it was her fear that was robbing her of her own power and with one last furious burst she made it, hurling them both inside the Morris.

"Get you, Daley Thompson," gasped Icarus, falling into the driver's seat, purple with effort. "Now what do we do?"

But Molly had her arms tightly around Floris and was weeping into his hair with relief. "He's safe," she sobbed. "We saved him. I can't believe we did it."

CHAPTER NINETEEN

The Battle

"I don't think we're home and dry yet," said Icarus, warning. But Molly, oblivious to everything but Floris, was wrapping him in Dorothy's old tartan rug like an outsize shawl, holding him to her, crooning wordlessly, willing her own warmth and strength to flow into the taut, chilled little body. His eyes flickered open, disturbingly vague, milky lenses that seemed not to see, then closed.

"Oh, Floris," she whispered, imploring, rubbing at his numb, bloodless hands and cheeks. "Please get warm."

"There's no time to fuss over him," Icarus hissed at her. He pointed unhappily. "Look! One minute they were all back there like shop-window dummies and then suddenly—*bing!*—they were down here. Without moving. Hollywood Special Effects."

Molly clutched harder than ever at the body of the ill child in her arms. The sight of the Magus of Harper's Ford flooded her with terror and rage. Before, at the roadhouse, he had been cold like ice, like iron. Now, in robes the color of dulled flame, he bore down on them like a searing desert wind that could parch and destroy everything in its path.

He has made himself quite mad with hating, she thought. I was right about that.

Behind the Magus, a tall young woman followed uncertainly, trailing folds of heavy gold cloth, her hair imprisoned under a jeweled cap. Mrs. Magus, thought Molly. Though she looks young enough to be his granddaughter. But there's no Master or Miss Magus. *How do I know that?* Behind the Magus and his frightened Lady came five or six young men with cropped hair and professionally bland faces above their close-fitting garments of harsh blue. *Apprentice wizards?* wondered Molly. *Or just henchmen? Heavies?*

It was at least some comfort to Molly to recognize, on the other side of Tin Witch, the sad and stormy Lady Agnes, her lion-haired husband at her side, incongruously wearing mud-stained hunting clothes as if he had been snatched by enchantment as he rode home weary and saddle-sore from the chase. Even though it was terrifying to be mixed up in such strange magical events, Molly felt curiously lulled by an increasing sense of familiarity, as though she was watching an old fairy tale unfolding to its only possible conclusion. The opposing forces were gathered: the dark powers ranged against the dazzling light. Then her stomach plummeted and she took in the brutal truth. Neither Lady Agnes nor Lord Magus were paying the slightest attention to their little son huddled with Icarus and Molly in the old Morris Traveler.

"Icarus—they aren't going to help us," whispered Molly in terror. It was like the worst nightmare she had ever had. "It's just us—against all of them." Icarus reached for her hand. "She wanted to save him—I know she did—but—Icarus, she's part of his danger!"

"We're in the middle of something very heavy here," he said softly. "Between the devil and the deep. I have the feeling these two noble families are about to settle some really sordid old scores."

As the two groups of antagonists advanced on each other, the atmosphere thickened tangibly. Gasping, Molly felt as if she were trying to breathe through soup. Their hatred was suffocating her.

"They can't get any closer to the car," said Icarus. "Look—"

In the darkness of the car park, Tin Witch's moonshine glimmer shone with a steady gentle brightness. One either side the warring families pressed closer, but with expressions of increasing bafflement, as the air resisted them like walls of transparent jelly.

"Perhaps they won't be able to hurt us," said Molly hopefully.

"Don't bet on it," muttered Icarus.

After several moments of bouncing himself grimly but unproductively off jelly walls, the Magus demanded in a loud, harsh voice: "Whose feeble conjuring trick is this?" He looked almost peevish, Molly thought, a peevish, obstinate, sick old man.

"It is none of my doing," called Lady Agnes across the bonnet of Tin Witch in a voice so charged with cold contempt you could have cracked paving stones with it. "I do not fear to meet you face to face, my *Lord Magus*." She pronounced his title as she might have spat out something particularly disgusting.

"Then you should do," called back the Magus. "For of the seven it is *you*, not I, *your* family, not mine, that has broken the Law. You should fear me as the instrument of the Law come to have justice."

"An evil law, Lord Magus. Perpetuating evil for seven hundred years. Has not Launde suffered enough?" Lady Agnes stood still as a pillar in her dazzling white gown, seeming to glimmer with her own cold light like a star. There were starry jewels braided into her loose bright hair. There was something dangerous, in the way she stood so still, as there had been something terrible in her dry-eyed grief at the loss of her child. As if something lay coiled and waiting at the bottom of a fathomless well, gathering power to strike.

"You do not know how to keep your Lady in her place," remarked the Magus of Harper's Ford to Lord Gilbert and as though Lady Agnes had not spoken a word. "It is as well that there are others in Launde who do."

His own lovely young wife stood beside him as though frozen, her eyes lowered. What a yes-woman, thought Molly in disgust. If she had any spirit she'd poison his stew.

"Do you think they've forgotten about us?" she whispered, still hopeful but not very.

Icarus only shook his head, glum. "I hate this stuff," he whispered back. "Listen to them all going on about the Law and suffering. All they want to do is hurt each other. They've got no real idea why they hate each other if you ask me—they've just

238

got into the habit of it and they'll drag in any old fairy tale and half-baked history to justify their side. It reminds me of my parents before they split up. They make me quite ill." He looked it. She squeezed his hand, wanting to comfort him.

Lord Gilbert had turned scarlet. He gripped his own fists tightly. "I do not have to account to you, Lord Magus," he said, and he sounded quite heroic. "You invoke the Law, but it is not the Law which lies closest to your heart, but vengeance. The House-hold at Harper's Ford suckles all its nurslings—aye, when it has any—on deadly old poisons. And why? Because two foolish young lovers once loved and died. And because of this my family has been ac-cursed and punished by your line for generation after generation. And the kingdom of Launde, which was once a wonder of the worlds, is now blighted and divided. A barren law, Lord Magus, for a bar-ren household."

"If the children of my Household suck the poi-son of old vengeance," hissed the Magus, like a very old, very deadly cobra, his face white as ash, "then your babes suck the milk of *shame*. For to be sibling to this *inhuman spawn* is to know the de-generacy of the tainted stock which once bore Dominis."

Molly was rocking Floris rhythmically in her arms,

her head bent over him so that she could not see
their faces full of hate. To shut out their voices,
their terrible voices, flinging ritual insults like mad
booming giants, she said in her heart again and
again: *I love you. I love you.*

"They're getting down to it now," whispered Icarus.
"I think they've finished with the niceties."

"They don't care about Floris," Molly whispered
back, shakily. "I hate all of them. Even *she* cares
more about their stupid old feud than she does
about Floris. I thought *she* loved him, at least. But
she hasn't even looked at him properly. She's his
mother but he might as well not have one—"

"How she cradles him," hissed the Magus, mocking,
intimate and terrible in Molly's ear. "Even though
in her heart she secretly dreads what he might really
be. Yet she fools herself he might *learn* from her
to be *warm and loving.* Shall I show her...?"

As though he knew some new terror was beginning, Floris briefly opened his eyes again. With sight-
less pupils that floated milky, unfocused as a new-
born's, he tried to look around him, whimpering.

"Oh please—won't *you* help him?" Molly begged
Lady Agnes, imploring, stretching out her hands,
quite sick with dread. But his mother, dazzling the
stale darkness with her white starry rays, neither
saw nor heard. Her eyes were fastened unshakably

upon the figure of the Magus, whose arm was now raised in an exaggerated gesture of power, his sleeves of dulled flame falling back from his knotted old man's arms, a parody of a wicked wizard in a pantomime.

Oh no. Oh my God, Icarus—he's changing again. He's changing....

Floris had been cold before, but now, within the warm protective circle of her arms, his small frail body of flesh and blood shimmered and flowed, changing before her horrified eyes into a child of ice, from who all human color had ebbed away: calm, angelic, sculpted as though in translucent marble. An ice Michelangelo.

The burning chill struck into every nerve of her body, traveling like icy lightning along every vein, yet she held on. Whatever the Magus did, she would not let him go. She would do the only thing that was left for her to do for Floris, hold him in her human arms and love him with all her guilty heart.

Except for a tiny muscle moving faintly in her cheek, Lady Agnes stood still as death. From all its bewildering, stormy, many-colored complexity, her life had silently and suddenly narrowed down to this single loathed object: a gloating, shrunken old man in robes of dull flame. Around her a cloud of power was inexorably forming. It seethed, it swarmed with its own deadly life like an overturned hive of white and glittering bees. To all else but the hypnotic figure in red, Lady Agnes had become deaf and blind. She was going to fight the Magus.

—But through his body! Molly realized in anguish, biting back the terror, the unbearable pain that screamed to escape her locked jaws, cradling the beautiful child of ice, searing her own tender flesh. They're going to fight each other through Floris! *What else have they always done, unknowing,* sang that fiercely impersonal song in her bones, as if a star resided there.—*But always before the battle was hidden, underground. Now the horror is out!*

The dead-cold weight of Floris was lightening in her arms. He was returning, warming, color flowing back into his limbs and clothing: Briefly he was with her, honeysuckle hair and violet eyes gazing at her, terrified, imploring, then he was gone again, whirling, changing, glowing, condensing, shrinking down and down—*burning!*

In her hands she held a fiery coal, charring her palms. She gritted her teeth against the agony. She shut her eyes against the lie. She filled her mind with Floris, the sight and feel of him. *I love you. I love you. They won't get you.* The pain was so bad she was near to screaming out with it. *I love you.*

But again he was changing, changing, flickering

into himself and out again. Icarus was saying something but she couldn't hear him. She wouldn't look at what they were doing to him now, though she felt his child's flesh and soft sweet-smelling hair becoming something heavy and dulled that dragged her arms down with its weight, something scaled, slow and slithering. *But I know it's you, Floris. It's you I love.*

Molly, Molly! Icarus was calling to her. But she must not think. If she started to think she might be tricked into letting him go the way she had before.

Under her clutching hands the scaled coils became warm: a pulsing, fast-beating heart. A wild shuddering of feathers. Her eyes flew open with the shock of the new pain, the hot flow of her own blood. The young eaglet in her arms was slashing at her hand with its curved beak, frantic to be free. *But I love you, Floris. I know this isn't you.*

Molly—they'll kill him! Icarus's voice broke into her mind urgently where she was trapped in her nightmare. *They are killing him. They're just getting warmed up—flexing their muscles. Playing to see who gets to be Best Wizard. They can turn him into anything they want. When they've worked through Tam Lin for Beginners what'll they do next? Turn him into Bubonic Plague and give him to someone? A guided missile, perhaps?*

Floris flickered briefly into her arms. His eyes were huge and agonized, his breathing harsh and rasping. *But what can I do?* she begged Icarus.

"I think—" he started.

But Floris was shrinking, changing, squirming in her arms, growing sleek brown hair, squeaking in fury, darting his head at her to bite her with his sharp, poisoned-yellow teeth.

"Oh," she moaned in horror, clinging to the enormous hideous rat. "Oh, Floris, I know this isn't you. I love—" But again he was changing, changing. "How will I bear it?" she screamed to no one. "Help me, what can I do?"

But then Icarus lunged across her body, grasping Floris roughly by the shoulder as he flowed, shimmering, back into his own form, struggling now for breath, his face and body soaked with perspiration, and wrenching desperately at Floris's jeweled earring, Icarus tugged it finally free of its fastening.

With a shattering and unearthly scream, Floris fell back into Molly's arms, lifeless.

In Icarus's hands the jewel pulsed once, twice, three times and then winked out, a colorless crystal.

"That!" Molly just managed to say, recoiling from it in dread. *"That* was what was changing him." She was shaking all over. "He wasn't the one who

was doing it. He wasn't *ever* the Change-Thinge," she said numbly, "it was *that*."

"I think it had sort of made itself part of him," said Icarus. "I don't think it could help it." He jerked his head to indicate Lady Agnes and the Magus. "It's taken the wind out of their sails, hasn't it?"

They stood astonished, wearing the faintly foolish expressions of people caught out in a game of musical statues when the music stops. Unused magic collected around their feet in sullen pools like oil. Molly would have laughed right in their faces if she had not been shaking so badly and feeling so sick.

"I just thought it might be the earring," said Icarus, looking very ill himself. "Every time he was Floris again, I kept noticing that crystal, and each time it looked worse and worse, changing into more and more horrible colors, growing bigger and more menacing-looking. I didn't mean—I was just trying to stop them killing him between them."

Molly was still shaking. She thought she might never stop. She wanted only to get away from these mad people who glimmered and towered in the stale darkness of the car park: grotesque shadows by nightmare candlenight.

"Start the car," she begged. "Let's get him out of this."

Icarus was already fumbling with the ignition. Neither of them said yet that, in saving Floris from the warring enchantment of the two families, they might have cost him his life.

But as Tin Witch roared into deafening life, the figures of the Magus and his crop-haired henchmen, which had seemed frozen forever like jammed machinery, began to run forward, their faces distorted with rage.

"I think Dorothy's stuff has worn off," said Icarus. "Or worn out."

Even as Icarus was putting the car into gear and easing her away, they were advancing. In a moment all the misdirected power and rage of the Magus was going to be turned on Tin Witch and her passengers.

"Icarus!" shrieked Molly, pleading.

"I'm doing my best, Moll. She's got cold from all the hanging about. The choke should—"

"They're catching up! Oh, what can we do?"

The car was moving faster now, increasing the distance between itself and its pursuers, but how were they going to make the turn that would have to bring them past the Magus again before they could get onto the down ramp?

Icarus put his foot down. He was going to try to

scorch past them as fast as he could safely go in such a badly lit confined space. "Get down as we go past!" he yelled at her.

"They haven't got *guns*, Icarus, for heaven's sake—they've got magic. Oh, Icarus—slow down!"

"I can't. I can't," he said helplessly, stamping the brake.

Tin Witch wouldn't turn. Something was wrong. She just kept going faster and faster. Far behind them, Lady Agnes suddenly ran forward, crying out like a dreamer struggling out of a dream, but a furious silver-haired figure barred her way. The Magus stretched out his hand, its stiff fingers contorted with power.

A wall of solid brick, on which Molly clearly saw the words TRACY LOVES KEV FOREVER, parted like paper.

Out into the darkness, now tinged faintly pink and green with dawn, Tin Witch sailed like a ridiculous, gaudy metal bird: out over the evil-smelling river. And down.

And then it was over.

CHAPTER TWENTY

The Healing of
the Heartstone

*They are in the octagonal room in the Tower within
sound of the sea. The room is full of shadows and the
dancing brilliance of firelight and candlelight. Now
and then there is an explosive flare as flames detonate
hidden traces of salt in the driftwood burning on the
hearth.*

*In this room there is only peace and hope. All anger
and fear were laid aside before they entered, but the
truth is they don't remember entering, seem always to
have been here, content and tranquil.*

*Floris lies in her arms, his cheek softly against hers.
He is warm to the touch, like a summer peach on the
tree, and she knows this warmth is not from the fire's*

heat. The old frozen snows he has carried in his heart all his short troubled life have finally thawed and drained harmlessly away. The enchantment is broken.

Icarus is with her, quietly looking at the flames. There seems no need for words, for explanations.

With them in the Tower are the three people Molly has always known with the same wordless knowing that knows the room as well as she knows her own secret, timeless self.

The old lady sits in the corner, working at a rather dull-looking woolen sock with a large needle that flashes, catching the candlelight. Though her face is partly in shadow, her eyes are as bright as her needle, fierce as a falcon's. Ridiculously attired in the disheveled-hen hat and some shapeless dreadful black garment, so old that its color has become a trifle mossy with wear, bent over her apparently innocent darning, she still seems as compellingly, unsettlingly magical as she did on the night she blew into Molly's life with the storm.

The young woman stands beside Molly, handing her a steaming beaker, which she takes and drinks from obediently. She can identify the flavors of lemon, honey, spices, and apples, but there is something else indescribable, something peculiarly belonging to this world, this place, the kingdom between two forests. The warmth of it sinks deep into her bones and also spreads outward in gentle, glowing, healing ripples that envelop her *heart and her mind. Now she has committed herself to return. They want her to. She has a place with them and work to do. She is one of them, the Unbelonging, who belong to no one world alone, but to all the worlds, traveling between them, keeping the old ways open, reclaiming what was known from beyond Time, and making it new over and over again within Time, for all Time.*

Icarus also drinks from the steaming pewter mug and their eyes meet as he does so. He speaks to her then but without words. He says: I've been here before, Molly, in dreams.

So have I, she says.

I'll remember it this time. When we get back.

We both will, she says. She turns then to the hawk-faced man who sits working at the table behind her in shirtsleeves. With careful precision he is removing a small piece of colorless crystal from the setting of an earring. She knows it now for what it is: the missing fragment of the Heartstone.

Why? she asks. Was it done on purpose? To hurt the family at the castle because the first Magus blamed Dominis for the death of his daughter?

Who knows? he answers her. All that can be said for sure is that somehow the lost shard of the Heartstone found its way, whether by accident, carelessness, malice or some more fateful intent, into the coffers of the Cas-

tle of the Forests and was made into an heirloom earring for generations of the sons of the castle to be given at their naming. This is living crystal, lonely for the Mother Stone from which it was exiled. Orphaned, broken, in pain, it longs only to be part of a living being once again and it tries with all its power to become so. But until it was returned to the Mother Crystal this could never be. Damaged, it still possesses the powers and gifts of the whole Heartstone, but in a wild, uncontrolled, distorted form. Only one other power—

Music, says Icarus, understanding. *Music lulled it. Soothed it.*

What will you do with it now? asks Molly. The hawk-faced man is turning the bright shard in his hand, his face both joyful and grieving all at once.

Return it to the Heartstone. So Launde can begin to journey toward healing.

She will want him back, says the old lady, without looking up from her darning. *She longs for him. He must return to take his place in his own family. Never think she acted as she did because she did not love him, Molly. Blinded love, grief, loneliness, can work a twisted cord which may make people mad and monstrous despite themselves.*

The Magus, says Molly, able to remember without fear, *here—it made him mad and monstrous too. He* tried to kill us. I thought he'd give up and let us go after Icarus grabbed the earring and stopped Floris changing. But he still wanted to kill someone just as badly as ever.

And now he himself is dead, says the young woman, settling herself beside the hearth, drawing her long legs up under her chin, her hair flowing back in the firelight like the wild mane of some wonderful dryad. No, there was no act of vengeance against him. When the enchantment was broken, so was his mad purpose, and so, in the end, was he. For in a healed Launde where all living things might live in harmony, there was no place for such a dark lord as he bitterly and mistakenly believed that he must be.

In her strange, glowing beauty the young woman is as radiantly alive, even in her stillness, as some magical forest rowan. But Molly feels the tingling autumnal current of sadness that suggests she too would secretly have liked the Magus's story to have ended differently.

At first I thought the Magus had cursed Floris, like Lady Agnes said, says Molly. But he just knew how to make use of the curse, didn't he? He didn't understand it. He was as helpless as any of them underneath.

The Magus of Harper's Ford was as helpless as any man that was ever in Launde, says the old lady, very sadly. And try as he might, he could never conceal that shaming truth from himself. The more learned he became, the more practiced in enchantments and sorcery, the more he terrified and controlled everyone around him, the more driven and terrified he himself became.

Terrified of what? asks Icarus, puzzled.

He was a mad, vengeful old man, when your paths crossed, Icarus, but he was once a fearful little child growing up in a dark, cold household, haunted by old feuds, old hatreds, old tales and half-truths that blamed all present woes on the family that had once borne Dominis. He grew up more like a forgotten ghost than a human child, dwelling among other ghosts and shadows: an unloved starveling, a neglected, lopsided thing that never knew the sun. Had he grown up in a household of unhappy farmers or jewelers or blacksmiths his fate might have been kinder, but he grew up in the drafty ancestral halls of dark and angry old magicians— all of whom had, of course, also sought power in their turn to disguise their secret dread, camouflage lovelessness, banish old ghosts, old famished shadows. As a young man he vowed he would be more powerful, darker, more angry than any of them—

But he could never be sure, says Molly. If he was—

Ah, yes—the old lady nods—some weak place unguarded. Some chink, some sly knothole through which another might one day glimpse the dreadful emptiness that tormented him. And the earring did turn Floris into a kind of mirror, Molly. You were right, in your

253

moment of despair. When you most doubted yourself, you most doubted Floris, didn't you? And that was how the Magus was able to use you to get to him.

But—what was the Magus so afraid to see in Floris? Just a lot of bottled-up childhood bogeymen, do you mean? Icarus sounds quizzical.

No—not quite that. Perhaps what he most feared to find in the Change-Thinge of Launde was that lost dark driven thing he himself had slowly become over the years—the full horror of his own thwarted, denied and blasted being. Could he have faced the terror of the truth, confronted it, then he might have changed and lived and become a part of Launde's great healing. But like his magician forefathers he had neither strength, courage nor love enough of himself for such work. And so he could get no rest until the "Evil Change-Thinge" was hounded, shamed, punished and penned up forever in torment. From generation to generation this terrible curse was reenacted. But it is finished. It is over. Launde will wake up to a new morning.

Outside the Tower, Molly's sorrow waits for her, an unwieldly, leaking bundle she must shoulder and carry home later. But in this place and for now, she understands the reasons for everything that has happened and the part she plays in it. She know she will not struggle against what is right and necessary.

She will come for him, says the old lady—but not yet.

Yes, says Molly. I know.

How will you explain to your mother?

I shall tell her the truth, says Molly peacefully.

The Keeper turns in his chair, smiling at Molly and Icarus with such affectionate understanding that she is warmed through and through as if she had drunk again from the pewter beaker. The singing in the room, which had been so soft and constant she was unaware of it, suddenly surges, trumpeting and golden, like narcissi bursting into bloom after a long winter. And the song in her body rises in answer like an inward sun.

Well, Molly, you undertook your quest, he says humorously. You broke the enchantment. You found what was lost. You mended what was broken. You faced danger for someone you learned to love. Will you ask nothing in return?

Molly looks down at Floris, perfect in his sleep. *Only to be allowed to come and see Floris sometimes, she says—and to remember who I am and what I'm for, and where I belong. If I may.*

The Three Keepers of Launde, the Watchers, look at each other: an unsettling old lady in a disheveled feather hat, her lap full of dull-gray darning; a young woman with a wild dryad's beauty; a hawk-faced man with a shard of orphaned crystal in his hand.

And you? says the old lady to Icarus, fierce as ever—

you helped Molly. Without you, what was begun would not have been finished.

The same as Molly, says Icarus, simply. Apart from that I think we'll just have to spin our own straw into gold.

He looks across soberly at Molly and she gazes back at him, understanding all that he has not said.

The singing in the room rises steeply. The firelight catches both the shard of crystal and a small, apparently repaired and brightly burnished model of stars, moons, planets, suspended around a central sun, so that curiously swirling patterns of glowing color begin to flash around the walls, slowly at first, as though an old-fashioned merry-go-round is beginning to move stars, moons, planets, spinning gradually faster and faster, brighter and brighter. Molly can no longer look, closing her eyes against the painful rainbow dazzle. . . .

Tin Witch was bumping up the unpaved road to Dorothy's Gingerbread House in the early morning. As he banged down a crate of empties on the back of his truck, the milkman gave them an odd look. Floris stretched in Molly's stiffening arms and yawned hugely like a cat. She blinked hard and rubbed her eyes, yawning herself. Icarus, looking disgustingly normal and wide awake, gave her a broad grin.

"So you're with us again, are you?"

"When did it stop being the dream in the tower and start being Tin Witch again?" she asked, peering around her, utterly bewildered.

He shrugged. "Search me."

"You just came round and found yourself *driving*?"

"Nope," said Icarus, maddeningly.

"Stop being Humphrey Bogart, will you. What *happened*?"

"Molly—I came round and found us parked ever so nicely but unconventionally in the park down the road by the duck pond. I personally haven't the faintest idea how we got there. I had a little tiptoe round the Witch to check her over for damage and there isn't a scratch or a dent on her that wasn't there before. Then I thought I'd better get her out of the park before anyone came along, so I started her up very quietly so as not to disturb you. And here we are. Unscathed. With the little florist."

"If there isn't a dent in the Witch, do you think there also isn't a huge gaping hole in the side of the Glory Hallelujah car park?"

"Seems like it, doesn't it?"

"But it *happened*. It's impossible. But it happened."

"You don't have to tell me. And do you know, all I could think of as we flew out over that stinking polluted river was—why did they have to call me

257

Icarus? Just *look* at the trouble it's got me into. But in such nice company," he added generously, his old beautiful smile back in place.

Floris had opened his eyes and was gazing first at Icarus and then up at Molly.

Panic seized her. Would he still know her? Worse, even if he did, wouldn't he hate her for the macabre horrors she had helped put him through? Had she healed him of one wound only to afflict him with a worse one, one that would cripple him invisibly for the rest of his life? Blinking rapidly and painfully, she looked away from the searching scrutiny of those huge violet eyes.

Gently Icarus tugged at her sleeve. "Look."

A small delighted smile was slowly dawning on the little boy's face, as if it had had a long, long journey from his heart to reach his eyes and at last his mouth. In a sudden quick movement he reached up and put his arms tightly round her neck, pressing his warm cheek hard against hers. Then he opened his mouth and closed it once or twice like a baby bird's. Then he opened his mouth again and very carefully and clearly he said something.

"Molly," he said.

And then he laughed out loud at her wonderful surprise and said it again.

CHAPTER TWENTY-ONE

The Shabby Little Kingdom

The sadness and loneliness that Molly knew to be waiting for her somewhere in her future, like a bald, gloating vulture which would seize her in its talons just as soon as she was alone, did not actually get close enough to strike for some time.

When she and Floris walked into the kitchen at Vine Street, Maureen was in a whirl of excitement and good humor. Sean was making fried-egg sandwiches for everyone in sight. Clifford was cleaning a huge pair of shoes on a very small sheet of newspaper so that the polish landed on the linoleum in oily black clots and streaks in all directions: but he was grinning from ear to ear.

"He's got a job," said Maureen. "Go on, tell her, Cliff."

"Bloke's offered to train me," said Cliff shyly. "To fix bikes, like. Starting next week."

"Just phoned him up out of the blue," Maureen almost sang, whisking washing out of the old machine and into her huge laundry basket. "Said they'd heard so well of him."

Molly beamed. Whatever the job meant to Maureen, she recognized that it seemed to have started something like the same process in Cliff that snatching off Floris's earring had done for Floris. For there he stood, her large, dangerous brother, laughing like an idiot. And the laughter began in his eyes which looked straight back at her, bright, flecked, Irish green-hazel like her own: triumphant, yes, but unmistakably friendly.

In the background, Henry Preece was banging things down and scooping things out of cupboards and into suitcases. He was doing this with a melodramatic and injured sulkiness, Molly noticed, which might have been more impressive if only everyone else in the kitchen had not been talking and laughing and joking so loudly and happily. Feeling almost sorry for him, Molly said in polite surprise, "Are you leaving us, Mr. Preece?"

"So it would seem," he ground out, then he

compressed his lips tightly as if he could not trust himself to say anything further without irreparable danger to his dignity.

He wasn't doing very well collecting up his possessions, Molly thought with concern, banging and crashing them about like that. He was going to damage them. Her heart was so inflamed and full of love for the whole world, since the return of Floris, that she even had enough love to spare for unlovable Henry Preece. Swooping toward him, she cried: "Oh, do let me help."

Startled, rearing back from her in both irritation and distaste, Henry Preece struck the back of his head sharply on a projecting cupboard door. Even then only a muffled groan escaped his frozen lips. In unusually compassionate silence, as though in a hospital or a church, the entire Gurney family watched as the rapidly paling ex-lodger packed up the remainder of his possessions and left their kitchen without another word.

"What did you do to him?" asked Molly, open-mouthed. "Why's he going?"

To her surprise it was Cliff who answered. "I told him to sling his flaming hook, last night," he said gruffly, spattering more shoe polish. "He was giving Mum a hard time because she didn't want to marry him. I told him we didn't want his money

261

now, thanks, now I'm earning and Mum's got a few hours helping out at the nursery at the Leisure Center."

"Leisure Center?" repeated Molly blankly.

"A woman on my course phoned up and said she could use some help," said Maureen. "Well, it's a start, isn't it? Dipping my toe in the water before I try to find out if I still know how to swim. That man made me so angry, Molly. I should really be grateful to him. Do you know what he called all this"—she gestured around, her red hair shining. " 'Your shabby little kingdom,' that's what he said."

"I reckon he thought he was going to be the shabby little king," put in Sean unexpectedly.

"Anything else I should know?" asked Molly, laughing but suddenly utterly exhausted, sinking down into a chair. "Has Sean got a job making fried-egg sandwiches for the United Nations or anything?"

All the time Floris stood beside her, gazing round the kitchen with his huge beautiful eyes, his hand tightly gripping Molly's. Maureen seemed to take them both in properly for the first time. "Well, what about you, Moll? You look better. Have you had a good time?"

"Tell you about it later," said Molly. It could

wait. Somewhere in the house her vulture hovered, waiting. Well, it could wait a bit longer, she thought.

He's lost his earring," Cliff said suddenly. "What you done with your jewelry, mate?" He ruffled Floris's curls, leaving a faint smear of shoe polish behind.

Floris opened and shut his mouth a few times experimentally. Then he grinned and opened his hands in a broad gesture, pantomiming emptiness.

"Gone," he said.

Molly tiptoed in to check on him that night and found him sound asleep, breathing softly, his cheek on his hand. Across the garden wall, deep amongst the wild orchard and the overgrown graves, she sensed the other household, his other family. The barrier between them was very thin now, like the translucent shell of some magical egg, thinning and thinning before it hatched. She knew if she looked what she would see. But when, swallowing from a tightening throat, she softly moved aside a corner of the curtain, she was not prepared for the sheer beauty of the ancient castle, floating in its haze of light like an enchanted island in the summer darkness.

She will come for him—but not yet.

"I know," she said aloud.

Whenever she woke in the night the castle in its floating haze was calling to her. Whenever she slept she saw the children, Minna, Orlando, Merlin, and Edward, running in and out of the great rooms, pounding down the twisting shadowy stairs where torches flared, calling to each other in high-pitched excitement:

"He's coming home! They've said so. They've promised. The enchantment is broken!"

"*She* doesn't sit and rock and stare at the wall—she was opening the windows in his room: She was singing."

"*He* says he'll take me hunting—he was laughing and they were holding hands in the garden. She splashed him with water from the fountain and he was *laughing!* I saw them."

"But when will Floris come home again? When will he?"

CHAPTER TWENTY-TWO

Voices in the Garden

Summer passed. It was time for Molly to tell her mother, but she didn't know how to begin. In the tower, in the safe circle of firelight, everything had been simple and straight. In the kitchen at Vine Street it was never the right moment. The mood was always wrong: too happy, too tired, too busy.

Gradually Molly realized she was only making excuses. Once she had told her mother then it would be true and inescapable, and from there it was only a short step to losing Floris forever.

She is coming for him.

I know, answered the music in her bones.

One early-autumn afternoon, she found Floris

in the garden, sitting quietly and solemnly with one of the cats, his favorite, Licorice. He wore an intensely yearning expression and Molly's heart caught when she saw it.

"What are you doing?" she said, too cheerful, too normal.

He turned toward her with eyes glistening with tears and he pointed at the crumbling wall that separated the little grassed-over yard from the brambles and arthritic old fruit trees of the orchard.

"Listening," he said. "Listening to them."

Listening hard herself, Molly could clearly hear Minna's giggle. She was teasing someone. She thought she could hear Orlando too. He seemed to be arguing with Merlin over a pocket knife. Their voices rose effortlessly over the orchard like bird-song, happy, quarrelsome, ordinary: Floris's noisy brothers and sisters.

"Soon," said Molly, hugging him hard. "I promise they're coming for you very soon."

He blinked at her, his eyes clear and beautiful, with none of the old bewildered hurt hidden behind them. Possessively he clung to Licorice, who submitted passively, purring and making her own peculiar, bleating double mew with the catch in it, snaking her small sleek head to appear foolish but adoringly under his arm, her whiskers stiff little wires, an idiotic cartoon cat.

"I take her," he said sternly. "My little cat."

"Yes," said Molly, her heart breaking. "You can take the cat. She loves you."

*   *   *

They're making a feast. You should see the great hall! They've put up garlands of flowers and a great tent of green branches—it's like an indoor forest!"

"Nan is whipping enough cream to make a mountain, and there's jellies and pies—and little bears of brown sugar and little pigs of pink. And there's going to be—you won't guess, ever!"

"What? Don't be silly, Eddie. Stand still and tell me," commands Minna, cool, imperious in her new frock of sapphire blue, sapphire ribbons braided into her corn-gold hair.

"Fireworks!" chortles Eddie, his cheeks flaming away like harvest poppies. "Real fireworks!"

And off they all race with a clatter of boots and buttoned shoes, down the echoing stone passages, whooping and shouting, their shadows flickering along the walls. Eddie (on a battered hobbyhorse with buttons for eyes and a missing ear), being the smallest and youngest, is the last to vanish. And Molly hears him call piercingly after the others as they careen madly in the direction of all the glorious sweet and savory kitchen smells—"And

*they say the Launde Players will come again like they
did in the old days. And everyone will dance until
sunrise. . . ."*

Molly woke. Floris was kneeling on his small bed,
fully dressed, outlined sharply in the moonlight that
spilled through the window. He had pulled back
the curtains. Then Molly saw that it was not moonlight that dazzled so brightly, but a pouring brilliance from the castle in the orchard, from which
also flooded sounds of laughter, music and merry-
making.

Under tiny fluffy clouds in a slight breeze, bright
flags fluttered. The celebration had begun. It was
time.

She groped her way to Maureen's room across
the dark landing only to find Maureen already
awake, coming blearily out of her door and putting on her dressing gown. "What's all the noise?"
she asked, blinking sleepily. "There's such a rac-
ket going on somewhere. Is someone having a
party?"

Silently Molly blessed the Keepers for making it
possible, this once, for Maureen to see and hear at
least this event in the kingdom of Launde.

"Come with me, Mum," she said, gently and

firmly taking her mother's hand. "It's Floris's mother and father. They've come to take him home."

Perplexed but unprotesting, Maureen let her daughter lead her downstairs to the kitchen, Floris springing ahead of them like a puppy, trembling visibly with excitement. Then, just as Molly turned the giant key that had been too large and heavy for his small hands, he remembered something and dived into Maureen's sewing basket by the heater, emerging with a purring armful of shadow that flexed itself into a cat shape, kneading his shoulders, sniffling and buttingly him lovingly.

"I take my cat," he explained solemnly to Maureen, holding Licorice tightly to his narrow chest.

"Are they out here?" asked Maureen, bemused, following them in a stumbling daze. Molly guessed she thought she must be dreaming.

There was a sharp frost. Their breath flew out before them in silvery plumes. Yet the light streamed over the garden wall as brightly as summer sunlight, and the sounds of merriment washed gaily over the little garden with its silvered coal shed and glitter-touched garbage pails like a wave. Haunting music: pipes and strings and drums. All along Vine Street the curtains remained tightly drawn: the houses dark, silent, sleeping, oblivious of enchantment.

Floris began to run over the whitened grass. Licorice had slithered out of his grasp and galloped beside him, her tail held high. Molly had puzzled over the next part. How it might happen. But it was breathtakingly simple when it came to it. As Floris ran forward, his sneakers crunching on frozen grass, the wall at the end of the garden simply dissolved, just as the car-park had once parted like paper for Tin Witch. And there, standing waiting for him, in all their jeweled and shining party finery, were his mother and father and all his six brothers and sisters, their faces smiling and joyful. Beside them, almost invisible in her tattered old black coat, was an old lady who nodded at Molly, her eyes full of fierce understanding. For a moment Floris halted and looked back at Molly, suddenly unsure.

"Go on, sunbeam," she encouraged him huskily.

Then he turned and hurtled onward, his arms held out. "Mama!" he cried. "Papa!" Onward into the dazzling light and the streaming music of Launde. And the wall closed after him. There was silence and freezing darkness as if a great door had slammed in their faces.

"He took Licorice," said Maureen, wiping something from her face.

And that was all either of them said.

CHAPTER TWENTY-THREE

The Present

Early summer in the orchard. Since no one seems to mind, Molly has taken to spending some time there now and then. She and Icarus sprawl under the apple blossom, sometimes reading, sometimes talking. Icarus is on a visit to his aunt Dorothy on a welcome weekend away from his college in London.

Then they hear a cat, bleating: a distinctive double mew with a catch in it.

"That's Licorice," says Molly sitting up. There is a rustle now, and a great deal of cracking of twigs and muffled giggles and what might be the sound of several small people retreating to a safe distance.

"I think they've left you a present," says Icarus,

pointing to something hanging, shining, in the apple tree amongst the freckled pink and white of the blossom. "You're going to have to climb up to get it."

As she cautiously climbs, wondering, up and up into the blossoming branches, she can hear Orlando stifling a giggle and she is sure that must be Minna whispering sternly to everyone else to behave and be sensible.

"I think this is a bit of lawn from Minna's dress," says Molly aloud. "And I'm sure this little strand of hair belongs to Floris." Looking down through the green lattice of leaves, she knows that he can see her: She can feel him fizzing like sherbet with suppressed excitement. She smiles. "Don't be hard on him, Minna. He's being as still as a mouse. You've really made me climb right up to the top, it's a good thing I'm wearing my— Oh!" Her voice changes. "Oh, it's beautiful! A tiny perfect apple with leaves and a stem—all made of crystal, on a golden chain. Oh, *look*, Icarus."

She jumps down beside him, scattering petals, tiny twigs and green flakes of moldering bark onto his dark curls and the pages of his book, the crystal apple humming and brightening in her hand like a live thing on its fine shimmer of chain.

"What kind is it, do you think?" she asks, showing it to Icarus. "What will it do? What is it for?"

Molly feels, light as fingers of sunlight, a small child's touch on her hair, daring, fleeting. Then more scamperings, squeakings, and then silence. For now.